SOMETHING BORROWED, SOMETHING BLOOD-SOAKED

CHRISTA CARMEN

Something Borrowed, Something Blood-Soaked by Christa Carmen
Paperback Edition: 978-1-989206-00-3

"This beautifully macabre collection of urban legends and ghastly encounters is a cold whisper, a dripping axe, a shattered camera lens. Walk carefully into Carmen's night. But if you hear flies, run."

—Stephanie M. Wytovich, Bram Stoker award-winning author of *Brothel*

"Christa Carmen is undoubtedly one of horror's most exciting and distinctive new voices, and her debut collection absolutely proves why. From hardcore to heart-wrenching, these tales run the gamut, with each one of them taking hold of you and not letting go. *Something Borrowed, Something Blood-Soaked* is one incredibly wild ride. Hold on tight."

—Gwendolyn Kiste, author of *And Her Smile Will Untether the Universe* and *Pretty Marys All in a Row*

"Christa Carmen's *Something Borrowed, Something Blood-Soaked* is a gorgeous foray into the dark inner world of her layered, complicated characters. Her beautiful, languid prose pulls you in from the first line and keeps you there, mesmerized as she vividly constructs a brand new universe around you:

'Your smiles are two gardens, and the moss-covered walls around them have begun to crumble.'

—Christa Carmen

Something Borrowed, Something Blood-Soaked is like a wild and thrilling roller coaster. At the end, you won't want to get off the ride but keep on going, over and over."

—Christina Sng, Bram Stoker award-winning author of *A Collection of Nightmares*

SOMETHING BORROWED, SOMETHING BLOOD-SOAKED

FOREWORD

Cold feet. The term used in conjunction with approaching nuptials covers all manner of anxieties about the big day, as well as the relationship itself. Though we like to consider "true love" our end-all-be-all motivation for joining our lives with another, there are innumerable reasons people seek relationships—and just as many reasons they run.

Try to pry that truth from your lover's lips, however, and you risk getting bitten. If there's anything we value more than the idea of true love, it's the need to protect our secrets.

But Christa Carmen isn't interested in silence, and her collection Something Borrowed, Something Blood-Soaked isn't looking to lead you calmly down the aisle. Your path is littered with temptations that test the strength of your mind, heart, and stomach, and over thirteen tales of death and dependency,

Christa Carmen has you questioning whether love is real or just another addiction.

Don't run, lovers. You can't. This aisle is warm and sticky and it's going to devour you from the toes up. By the end of this collective ceremony, you'll never have cold feet again.

Jessica McHugh

THIRSTY CREATURES

The trees were fire and the sky was panicked birds and the horse was made of bone.

She knew the horse would not walk forever. She also knew that when the horse could go no farther, she would trade her Hell on Earth for one beyond her capacity to conceive.

—

On the day the water turned to poison, she had done the bad thing again. When her father appeared before her, she was certain it was to scold her for her atrocious, perverted ways. But when her father opened his mouth, a river of red ran out in place of reproach. In a revelation of horror, she remembered her father guzzling the glass of water from the faucet, and she gripped her favorite stuffed creature—a gift that she had not deserved—as the gore rushed from between her father's lips, hiding her face in its fur so she would not have to see.

She heard the muffled thwump when her father's body hit the floor. By then, her brother had drunk the water too,

(*by then, who hadn't?*)

and when he saw their father in a frothy sea of unrelenting red, he opened his mouth to scream. His insides came out instead of sound.

She watched as the mundane setting of their living room became an estuary of brackish blood, her brother's red mixing with her father's. The book that had taught her about brackish water and estuaries and other interesting, scientific things lay open on her desk upstairs. It would remain there now, for an eternity. Unless the water cleared and there was anyone left to drink it.

When the bottled water had been reduced to a wasteland of empty plastic, she braced herself to venture outside. Outside, where the world rained ash and the wind blew pain. It was also where the well ran deep, and if she was lucky, ran clean.

She was desperate for a drink, but recalled the book on her desk, extolling the scientific method and the testing of hypotheses. With her tongue like a shed carapace in her mouth, and her innards like sand in a sieve, she crouched behind the stone wall and settled in to *observe*.

When to delay another second would be a fate worse than what waited for her in the kitchen tap, a raven fluttered down to perch on the bait: a bucket of water exhumed from the well's depths. The great black bird lowered its head to sip, and splashed water over its wings. She held her breath, waiting for a rivulet of red to spew from its throat, to wrack its fragile, feathered body. The raven opened its beak, but only a song emerged, and she wept with relief. The salty tears made her thirstier than ever.

She filled every container she could find with unspoiled water from the well. An old tomcat mewled and hissed and spat, and though she lamented his misfortune, she could not share such a precious commodity with a cat. She reminded herself that she was wicked and depraved, and this allowed her to stomach her cruelty more easily.

She carried bucket after bucket of crisp, cool water to the barn, delivering the stores to a single stall. Encompassed in the narrow space was her father's former show horse, the strongest horse on the farm, of the most impressive breeding. The horse that would fare the best when it came time to abandon their home.

Without water, the milk cow and the donkeys and the other horses fell. Their already dehydrated corpses withered and shrunk, their eye sockets widening to gaping, fly-infested chasms. She was not privy to the noises their bodies made when they collapsed, but she imagined they sounded like her father had. Like her brother. All things sounded the same when they fell in death.

The morning the well ran dry, the air was thick and smelled of sulfur. She tacked up her mount and filled the saddlebags with bottles and canteens. She left the farm, not bothering to say goodbye. She did bring along her favorite stuffed creature, holding it before her on the horn of the saddle. A sleight of hand to delude herself into believing she did not ride alone.

The earth was blood red and bone dry. She saw no one in the weeks and months after setting out, would have almost welcomed the inconvenience of defending her water supply from fiend or foe. With no one to contend with, the caches of hydration were infinite; abandoned grocery stores reigned over empty parking lots, and households were rife with bottles of uncontaminated liquid, foregone by the fallen for the poison-spouting spigots.

There were no budding blossoms or kaleidoscopic foliage with which to judge the passing of the seasons. The horse had long become accustomed to the endless road, its body changing, shifting, ridding itself of useless things like tissue and muscle and flesh. Now the once-show horse was a chrysalis of dust and bone, its ribcage a steel trap that held its heart hostage.

Her own skin had fused with the horse's hellish hide. She had ridden the wretched beast to the ends of the Earth and back, and would repeat this journey over and over, with no end in sight. The stuffed creature, too, persisted, its body worn to nothing by the friction of her hands, its face erased by kisses from parched lips. It was a tether to the past and a clue to her future. The faceless, nameless being, a blueprint for her soul.

At first, she prayed to the deities of water, of wells and springs and fountains and rivers, and to the god and queen of the sea. She pleaded with them to release her as they had all the others. But she knew that to pray was to sin, for she knew her punishment was just. It was her fate to have all the water in the world, and no way to douse the fire.

Time disintegrated, and it came to her that she had not required a drink in as long as she could remember. Somewhere along the purgatorial path, she had ceased to possess those qualities that made her human. Water was no longer essential. As it were, every drop had long since dried up. Her thirst, however, was torturous and vast.

If she could only take back the bad thing, she'd have done so in a heartbeat. She would have drunk the poisoned water in her brother's place a thousand times over, and the river of red would have poured from her mouth in place of all her lies.

But...

The trees were fire and the sky was panicked birds and the horse was made of bone.

And she was one with the horse, an empty web of regret. Like the stuffed creature in her arms, her last link to a long-gone world, she was faceless. Formless.

And so very, very thirsty.

RED ROOM

The flash that dissolved the alcohol-sodden trappings of Marci's hangover-cocoon was blinding white and machine-gun sharp. Marci flinched, still half-asleep, and tried to shield her eyes from the onslaught.

"You legit look like the Bride of Frankenstein," Caleb said. He stood over her with cell phone in hand, snapping photos and looking grotesquely pleased with himself.

Marci mumbled something incoherent, and explored the straw-stiff ropes of hair that had prompted Caleb's observation. In addition to her *coiffure à la electrocution*, she felt at least two bobby pins she'd overlooked the night before, jabbing her scalp through the hairsprayed strands like the pincer claws of hard-shelled bugs.

Another flash went off, and Marci propped herself up on her elbows. "Can you knock it the fuck off?" Her tone was mirthless. "I appreciate that my hair has whipped you into a photographic frenzy, but I'm nauseous enough from all the

Fireball consumed last night that the presence of strobe lights in our bedroom can only hurt matters."

She groped around the nightstand before realizing that the cell phone Caleb held was her own. "Give me that. Why are you using my phone anyway?"

Caleb tossed it over without answering. She thumbed the phone to life, dimming the too-bright screen before commencing her morning routine of email checking and Facebook perusing.

Caleb flopped onto the bed and chugged from a giant bottle of water. "Goddamn. That was some party. Good thing we didn't have far to drive home." He rolled toward Marci and watched as she scrolled past pictures already posted from his sister's wedding the night before. "Did you get any good ones?" He snatched the phone back and opened the photos app. "You should post one of us. You know... a preview for our own wedding in a few months."

Marci's lips pursed, but Caleb was already scrolling, and quickly at that, past shots of pastel-bedecked bridesmaids, his sister in a white satin robe with *Bride* emblazoned on the back in glittering sequins, his fiancé flanked by two hairstylists for what would later become her morning-after-Bride-of-Frankenstein-'do. He passed over photos of the ceremony with equal amounts indifference, but slowed when he got to the first of the shots from the reception, scanning the frame for a glimpse of his own, tuxedoed self.

Marci pried the phone from Caleb's fingers and gave him a stony look.

She scrolled until she reached a photo of the wedding party on the front steps of the resort. Several of the bridesmaids had danced themselves into hairstyles that rivaled Marci's current one, the men had all loosened their ties, and the best man and maid of honor flanked the group on either side, champagne bottles held to their lips, fists raised in celebration of a wedding done right.

"Yup," Marci said with a bitter little laugh. She grimaced at the full-to-the-brim martini she clutched in the photo. "Despite the personal bad decision to over-imbibe, that's a pretty memorable shot to have ended the night on." She looked, suddenly, as if she might be sick. She pressed her arms to the mattress in a feeble attempt to stop the room from spinning, and mouthed, *don't throw up, don't throw up,* as if those words were the trick to undoing the damage wrought by too much vodka.

"You're a real hurtin' doobie, aren't you?" Caleb asked, a strange sort of glee suffusing his features. "That makes the pics I just took all the more valuable. Let's see 'em." He reached for the phone but stopped short, eyeing her intently. "You know, Bride of Frankenstein isn't quite right. You actually look more like Medusa."

"Gee, thanks," Marci said. She pulled the phone closer to her chest, out of Caleb's reach.

"Aw, come on." Caleb wrapped his hands around the back of her neck and tried to pull her in for a kiss. "Let's see how frisky you and your snake-hair can be."

Marci squirmed from his grasp and rolled onto her side. "What part of hungover don't you understand?" She punched in the phone's passcode and navigated back to her photos. "One more move like that, and this Medusa will have no choice but to turn you into—"

22

The word died in her throat like a snake whose head has been severed by a garden shear. She stared at the image on her phone. Shock and confusion etched her corpse-pale face; the sooty remnants of her makeup ringed eyes as big as saucers.

In the space between the last wedding photo of the night, and the ones taken by Caleb that morning, was a picture of a room. At first, Marci hadn't realized that the cause for the room's overwhelmingly red hue was the veritable sea of blood that covered its floor and walls. Once she'd overcome this optical hurdle, it was Marci's sense of reality that had to grapple with what she was seeing; this image of carnage that couldn't be so.

A single bare bulb lit the room, hanging from the ceiling by a twisted piece of wire. An old-fashioned claw foot tub menaced from one corner, though the room couldn't reasonably be called a bathroom. The room couldn't reasonably be called anything, really, except perhaps an abattoir, saturated like it was, and seemed always to have been.

The tub was full of blood. Marci could see that it had overflowed, spilling its crimson contents onto the crimson floor. Blood dripped from the ceiling like seething, poison rain, where the arterial spray of the room's victims had left not a single patch of plaster unstained. A row of jagged surgical instruments gleamed red from a blood-drenched counter and the man in the center of the photo's frame wore a blood-speckled mask of singular concentration.

The man in the foreground of the photo held something disinterestedly between gore-smeared fingers, a wet mass of blood-tinged hair, the scalp still clinging, thin and fragile-looking, like dampened tissue paper that will tear and clump at the lightest touch.

There was a third subject in the photo.

Stacked in separate piles of limbs and organs on a bloody wooden chair thread with a rusty chain, flesh pared from bone, skin from muscle, wet, yellow fat marbling meat.

Marci sucked in a breath. "What the fuck?"

Curiosity piqued at the shock in Marci's voice, Caleb craned to regard the screen. "What?" he asked. "What is it?"

Marci angled the screen so Caleb could see the gruesome image. "It's at the end of all the wedding photos, but before the ones you took of me this morning." She tapped the photo to bring up its details, squinting at the timestamp in the upper center of the frame. "It was taken at three twenty-eight AM."

She scrolled back a photo. "The picture on the steps of the hotel was at one twenty-six." She stared hard at Caleb. "How did it get on my phone?"

Caleb's expression of surprise was almost cartoonish. "What do you mean? How do you think it got there? You must have fallen asleep with the phone in your hands and screenshotted something you were scrolling past on Facebook."

Marci looked momentarily relieved as she considered this. She reanimated the phone, which had fallen dark, and inspected the mysterious photo. "It can't be a screen shot," she said, pulling up Facebook for comparison. "If it was, there'd be text, or a white border around it, and there's not."

"Then you screenshotted it from a Safari browser or

something. I don't know, Mar. What's the alternative? That someone snuck into our bedroom after we fell asleep, took your phone, snapped a photo of a room covered in blood, and returned the phone to your nightstand without either of us waking up?"

He slid from the bed and stretched, the t-shirt he wore riding up on his stomach. Marci turned away from the exposed skin. "Maybe someone uploaded it to your phone at the reception as a joke." he continued. "Or there was a glitch in the iCloud and some stupid still from a bad horror movie ended up on your phone."

With one quick motion, he flung open the curtain on the slider door. Sunlight glinted through the slats of the deck and fell across the master bedroom. Marci shrank from the bright light and moaned.

"I need a coffee," Caleb announced, ignoring Marci's distress. "Or better yet, a Bloody Mary." He moved toward the door.

When Marci did not follow, Caleb looked back, derision marring the conventionally-handsome features. "Forget about the picture, Mar." His fingers drummed against the doorframe. "Or, don't forget about it. Tell everyone at the BBQ today how you fell asleep with your finger on some torture porn site, accidentally saved it to your phone, and got all paranoid that someone was out to get you."

He turned and started down the hall, humming some tune he'd cut a rug to the night before, and chuckling to himself.

—

The second photo appeared one week later, discovered when

Marci went scrolling through photos of her overweight cat over her morning tea and toast. The timestamp on the image read *3:19 AM;* the red room was at the end of a long, dark hall and the two men from the first photo were present once again.

They dragged something along the ground, a body that, where the black-red patina of light from the room ahead did not extend, was shrouded in shadow. It was the flash of the camera that illuminated the captive's hands and feet, bound by rope, the layers of tape wound tight behind the head. There were no clues as to the photographer's identity; neither did it seem likely that the captive would find reprieve from his or her trip toward the red room before… what? Before they met their fate of being chopped into pieces, their blood used to bathe the walls as thickly as newly-applied paint?

Marci found Caleb playing Xbox on his throne: the worn leather armchair of the living room.

"Look," she said, shoving the phone under his nose. She took a deep breath and held it, quelling the slight trembling of her hands.

Caleb batted at her arm, his voice rising in anger. "What the fuck, Marci?" He threw the controller onto the coffee table, where it upset a framed photo of the two of them on vacation in Hawaii the previous year.

"It's a video game," Marci said. "Unending lives at your disposal. I *need* you to look at this. Another picture appeared. The same two men are in it, only, I swear it was taken just *before* the one I got last week. I think it's a photo of someone being dragged down the hall toward that

26

horrible room. It's like... it's like I'm getting clues to a murder in the opposite direction or something."

Caleb choked on the soda he was guzzling. "You're joking right? Even if that wasn't completely ridiculous, I saw on the news that there was a worldwide cyber-attack last week. Major corporations from pharmaceuticals to the tech industry got hit." He slammed the can down on the coffee table. "Your iCloud got hacked, simple as that. I don't understand why you're hell-bent on playing Nancy Drew."

"Because I didn't get hacked!" Marci protested. "I know I didn't. Something about these photos seems real. Call it a hunch, or female intuition, or whatever you want to call it, but it's like I know something bad is going to happen if I don't figure out where these photos are coming from."

Caleb unearthed his phone from a crack in the armchair and typed with quick, furious jabs. He turned the screen toward her, and Marci watched the news site load, saw the headline proclaiming, "Global Ransomware Attack: What We Know and Don't Know."

"Call Apple," he said. "Call them right now so we can put this thing to rest."

Marci returned her attention to the picture on the coffee table. When she spoke, she dispensed with each word carefully, as if laying stones to cross a rushing river. "Why don't you believe me?" She lifted her eyes to meet his. "You never believe me. You didn't believe me when I told you I was happy not being married. You didn't believe me when I said I could be committed without wearing a ring. And you don't believe me about this."

She stood before he could answer, and collected her purse

from the back of a chair. "I'm going to the police station," she said. "To show them the photos." Caleb tried to interject, but she cut him off. "I'm going, Caleb. End of story. Who knows... maybe they'll believe me."

—

Caleb was back on his throne when Marci returned, though he'd traded the *Resident Evil* video game for an equally sinister-looking horror movie. Marci walked past him with no intention of stopping when he lowered the volume and said, "Don't be mad at me, Mar."

She paused, and turned to look at him. "I'm not mad."

"What did the police say?"

Marci sighed. "They asked if it was possible someone was playing a joke on me. In other words, they believed me about as much as you do."

Caleb at least had the diplomacy to feign being sympathetic. "You want to come watch this movie with me? It just started."

Marci wrinkled her nose. "No, thanks. I'm going to bed." The sound of ramping-up horror revving its engine came from the speakers and Marci turned to watch the action unfolding on the screen.

"Shocking," she said after a moment. "A woman trying to convince a cabin full of people they're all gonna die and no one believes her."

—

Marci woke in the blackest part of night. She was short of breath, suggesting some nocturnal torment that had fragmented upon waking, and her t-shirt was damp. She reached out, but only rumpled sheets were present where

Caleb should have lain. She listened for the telltale sounds of the television from the living room, but the house was still, airless, mausoleum-quiet.

Until it wasn't.

A noise; the creak of a floorboard from inside the closet.

All the details Marci had missed in her post-nightmare disorientation became apparent, then; the motionless ceiling fan that had been on when she'd gone to bed, the blank face of the alarm clock, the black pit outside the slider where a floodlight should have burned.

"Gizmo?" Marci whispered. But no corpulent cat materialized from the open closet; rather, another creak, followed by the very distinctive, very human sound of someone releasing a deliberate, measured breath from amongst the dress clothes and winter sweaters.

Fear driving her to recklessness, Marci darted a hand from beneath the sheets and felt around the nightstand for her phone. Her heart beat like a spooked herd of horses, but amongst the mound of books, the Kindle with its textured purple cover, the dish of rings and earrings, the bookmarks and pens and empty seltzer cans, there was no phone to be found.

Reaching further from the sanctuary of the covers, her breath coming in shallow gasps, Marci turned the switch on the bedside lamp—once, twice, three times—to no avail. She'd replaced the lightbulb mere weeks ago. The power was definitely out.

The sound of a wire hanger sliding over metal rod, and panic overtook her. Marci bolted from the bed and tried to scramble for the door. Her foot caught in the tangled bedsheets and she hit the floor hard, a yelp emanating from some primal place within her and escaping through trembling lips. More hangers slid across the rod, like nails on a chalkboard, or a coffin grinding against steel planks as it's lowered into the ground. She got her feet beneath her and tore from the room, her footsteps muffled on the hallway runner as she ran for the living room and the prospect of Caleb's aid.

Through the kitchen and into the living room, where the flicker of the television had been doused when something (or someone) had tripped the powerline. Marci rushed forward, whacking her thigh on the couch in the dark, repeating Caleb's name over and over until Caleb woke with a start.

"What's going on?"

Marci could see the general outline of his body in the haze of the open curtains, saw that he was in his boxer shorts and little else, his skin sheened with the thin layer of sweat that came with falling asleep on the uncomfortable leather couch.

"There's someone in the house," Marci whispered. "They took my phone. They're waiting in the closet, and the power's out."

Caleb's sleep-slowed brain kept him from registering her words and he stared at her, perplexed.

"Caleb!" She shoved him to get his attention. "Did you hear what I said? There's someone in the bedroom. My phone's gone."

Understanding flickered across Caleb's pillow-creased face.

"There's someone in the house!" she repeated.

Caleb shook his head, clearing the last of the cobwebs of sleep, before lumbering into the kitchen and rummaging in a drawer for a flashlight. Makeshift bludgeoning device in one hand, he slid the butcher knife from the block on the counter with the other.

"In the bedroom?" he clarified.

"Yes," Marci whispered back.

With clumsy steps of exaggerated stealth, Caleb crept down the hall, Marci following close behind. The hallway seemed to go on forever. Marci wrapped her arms around her t-shirt-clad torso to keep from shivering.

A pronounced *crack!* came from the room ahead. Both Caleb and Marci froze.

"What was that?" Caleb asked. He sounded little more than eight years old.

"I think it was the slider door slamming shut," Marci whispered.

They remained rooted in place another ten, twenty, thirty seconds. When no further sound came, Marci poked Caleb in the ribs and he lurched forward. They traversed the final three feet with Marci clutching the hem of Caleb's shirt, Caleb's shaky grip on the flashlight causing the strobe to tattoo wild patterns on the closed door before them.

"Did you shut the door?" Caleb asked.

Marci shook her head, eyes wide. They held each other's gaze a moment longer. Marci moved close, and whispered in Caleb's ear, "I'm scared." He only looked at her in reply, the whites of his eyes the most pronounced thing in the reflective glow of the flashlight. Marci reached out and gripped the doorknob. Caleb nodded his acquiescence, holding both flashlight and knife aloft, and Marci turned the knob and pushed open the door before she could change her mind.

The heretofore useless lamp at Marci's bedside turned on at once, throwing the room into brightness. The clock radio came to life, blaring music at an impossible volume, the English synthpop band, The Human League: "*Don't... don't you want me? You know I can't believe it when I hear that you won't see me...*" The manufactured piano chords and eighties techno beat plunged the room into something surreal, a scene from a home invasion horror film, the characters so distracted by the too-loud music they don't see the masked men sidling up to the slider door.

Marci spun to regard the curtainless slider. There was no one there.

Caleb shouted, "Turn this shit off!"

"You turn it off!"

"There's no one in here, Marci!"

"There was someone here before! I know there was!"

"Oh yeah? And they took your cell phone too, did they? Took your phone to snap more of their scary fucking pictures? Then why's your phone on the fucking nightstand, Marci? Why's it right fucking there where you put it?"

Marci was about to yell back when she saw her phone, perched atop the mound of books where she'd left it to charge the night before. Nevertheless, she persisted. "The phone *was* gone. The power was out! I heard someone breathing in the closet, pushing the clothes aside to make his way into the room. Why won't you believe me? They've been sneaking in, taking pictures to document the horrific tortures they've inflicted, have targeted me next, and you won't believe me!"

Caleb circled the bed and snatched up her phone, brandishing it at her like a weapon. "I don't believe you because you're fucking nuts, Marci. Paranoid, hysterical, and nuts."

He withdrew several steps, his back to the slider, still waving the phone as if he were trying to get the attention of a dog or a small child. "The pictures were some goddamn glitch, the things they showed weren't real, no one's out to get you, and most importantly," he threw the phone at her, and out of reflex, she caught it, "you're out of your fucking mind!"

The glass pane shattered behind him in a shrieking blast, the imploding glass shooting into the room with such ferocity that Marci didn't immediately realize a pair of black-gloved hands shot forward too. Out of the dark and into the room, they circled Caleb's chest and pulled him back so suddenly, the only thing he had time to do was drop the knife.

The second man stepped forward, boots crunching over shards of glass, the sound melding with the maddening blare of music and the screams Marci hadn't realized she'd been emitting. He swiped the flashlight from Caleb's hand and bashed him dispassionately over the head. Caleb went limp in the first man's grip. The second man grabbed Caleb's legs, and together, they carried Caleb off the porch and into the night, the hoot of an owl punctuating their disappearance.

By the time Marci had stopped screaming and rushed out

onto the deck, there was nothing visible beneath the moonlight but cold, black pavement and the cold, black void of a night that had swallowed Caleb up.

—

The last police officer had departed at four AM, leaving Marci to steal a few hours of fitful sleep on the living room couch, as far away from the boarded-up slider door as she could get.

Caleb was gone. The police had found no trace of the intruders, but were at least obliged, now, to take Marci's concerns over the photos seriously. She retrieved her phone from the coffee table, where it sat beside the frame she'd righted before falling asleep. Marci had thought the police would have taken the phone as evidence, but the young officer had been satisfied with Marci sending the files to his department email address for analysis.

Marci scrolled through the images again, searching for something she might have missed, some clue to the location of the red room, or the identities of the men who'd come for Caleb. When she reached the final photo, she backed out a screen. There was an additional photo, waiting, unviewed. Marci peered over her shoulder, but the big bay window harbored neither cryptic shadow nor alien shape. With shaking fingers, Marci opened the photo.

The red room's inflamed hue seemed to have grown redder with the grease of fresh blood. The room's newest occupant sat in the red-slicked tub, against the red-washed wall, where black-red plasma dripped from the ceiling, and rose-red lakes covered the floor. The space where the victim's head had been was red gore, and red muscle, and other red things that glistened and twitched in the red room's light.

Caleb's head sat atop the chair, splintered bone where the vertebra had severed setting him slightly askew, waiting as one of the men assembled glittering rows of silver-red tools, the only objects not entirely red in the expanse of red-swathed room. Even the man's dark clothes simmered red in the fever-dream miasma of the swinging bare bulb.

The second man was absent from the shot, having been enlisted to aim the camera.

The expression on Caleb's face was one of immense pleading.

His eyes said, *I'm sorry I didn't believe you...*

SOMETHING BORROWED SOMETHING BLOOD-SOAKED

The fire gave an inviting crackle as Bella's new husband locked her in a fervent embrace.

Bella pulled back. "We should get going. Everyone will be wondering where we are."

"Chill, Bel," Luke said. "No one expects the bride and groom to appear right after the wedding. Besides," he pressed his face obnoxiously into the bodice of her gown, "it's your fault we're so late."

Bella pulled away again and started across the lobby of The Stanley Hotel, catching her reflection in the window along with dozens of candle-lit Jack-o'-lanterns. *This should feel romantic,* she thought as Luke pushed past her out the door. *And anyway, it wasn't my idea to spend the last hour trekking to the edge of the forest with such a heavy load.*

Ghost hunters peppered the patio, wielding EMF meters and handheld audio recorders like picket signs, hoping the historic hotel would cough up a paranormal phenomenon. *Maybe this will be their lucky night.* Bella didn't believe in ghosts, but if anyone was stubborn enough to come back and haunt The Stanley's halls, it would be Aunt Louise.

At the concert hall, a wart-nosed witch took their tickets. "Oooh!" she squealed. "You're the bride and groom who were married here this afternoon. And how cute! You've covered your wedding dress and tuxedo with blood for your costumes." She squinted at them over the ticket booth. "It looks so real!"

"Right," Luke laughed. "Now we're Corpse Bride and Groom!"

Bella looked down at her dress. The splatters of blood were such that she could never have duplicated the pattern a second time. It called to mind the incomprehensible squiggles of her great-aunt's account ledgers, and Bella's feeling of powerlessness the day she'd announced her engagement to Luke. Louise's response: "Married! To a boy with the Devil in his eyes?"

Louise had been a hard woman to live with, but she was the only family Bella had. It had been like razors to her wrists when Louise had proclaimed Bella dead to her, and snapped the ledger shut in her face, never to open it again. Until...

Until Luke insisted that this was the only way. If he hadn't, I never would have gone to such extremes. I loved Aunt Louise.

"What are we going to do if someone asks where Aunt Louise is?"

Luke scoffed. "She's, like, a hundred years old, Bel. Everyone will think she's in bed. Anyway, we can't control the appetites of murderous ghosts. Just like we can't control the bears that stalk the borders of the national park." He winked, and Bella forced a heartsick smile.

"Come on," Luke said, grabbing Bella's hand, "let's dance."

Bella let Luke pull her into dips and twirls, the blood-stained dress billowing out around her. *He's been pulling me around since I said I do,* she thought wearily. *No, he's been pulling me around since the moment I let him treat me as something of a dirty joke instead of like a full human being. I should have listened to Aunt Louise in the first place.*

A chill swept through the room, raising the hairs on Bella's bare arms.

What did I always tell you, Belladonna? The harsh, unearthly voice was unmistakable even in the din of the masquerade. *Men should think twice before making widowhood women's only path to power.*

Bella smiled a smile more radiant than any captured by her wedding photographer.

It looked like those ghost hunters would have another specter to pursue after all.

SOULS, DARK AND DEEP

The doorbell rang.

Annie skidded to a halt in socked feet and batted her sister's hand from the knob. "I'll get it," she said, her smile smug.

Abigail frowned, but stepped back so Annie could open the door.

The stranger stood, illuminated by the fluorescent glow of the porchlight, rain dripping off the black slicker that hung down past her knees, red rubber boots shining wet on the welcome mat, her face disfigured by shadow.

"Hi," Abbie chirped.

Annie's glare had the desired effect; Abigail closed her mouth so fast, her teeth clacked. "Hi." Annie puffed out her chest. She stepped back to allow the stranger passage into the foyer. "I'm Annie. My parents will be right down. Come in."

No sooner had the hooded figure crossed the threshold than footsteps sounded on the landing above, and a silvery voice called out, "That must be Belinda!"

Maggie Townsend appeared at the top of the stairs, first as a sleek pair of satin high heels, followed by the swinging hem of a long navy dress. The final few steps saw the picture coalesce, and Annie admired the vintage cameo at her mother's throat, the perfectly-coiffed French braid draped over one shoulder.

"Come in out of that rain! Girls, give Belinda some room for heaven's sake." She held out one freshly-manicured hand for the babysitter's coat. "Did you find the house okay? I could have kissed Angela for putting me in touch with you this afternoon. You're a lifesaver. An absolute lifesaver."

Belinda slipped off the wet coat and handed it to her employer. She turned to the two girls, her expression grave. Then, she smiled a crooked smile, like a marionette whose mouth had been outfitted with only half its strings.

"So," Belinda said, "if you are Annie..." her eyes flicked left to right, "then *you* must be Abbie."

"Right!" Abbie said, thrilled to be addressed directly, insulated from her sister's reproach. "We have a new movie to watch, just so you know. It came from Amazon this morning. It's called *Moana*, and my friend, Tara, said it's really good, and—"

"All right, Abbie," their mother said, laughing. "I'm sure Belinda will watch a movie with you, if you ask her nicely." She turned and called up the stairs. "Come on, Paul! We're going to be late!"

Annie lagged as her mother led Belinda into the kitchen. She stared at the sleeve of the black rain slicker visible through a crack in the closet. She thought she'd seen something red when her mother had taken the babysitter's coat, a flash of liner, perhaps, or her eyes playing tricks with the blood-red hue of Belinda's boots.

"The girls' dinner is ready," her mother was saying as Annie entered the kitchen. "Just throw it in the microwave whenever. There's popcorn in the cupboard for the movie and you can help yourself to whatever you'd like."

The dark-haired, dark-eyed girl nodded. "Thank you."

Abigail was staring at Belinda with the unabashed interest of a six year old, her eyes coming to rest on the front of her black smock.

"Your dress has pockets!" she exclaimed. "Neat!"

"Lots of dresses have pockets," Annie pointed out.

Abigail ignored her and twirled around the kitchen, spinning in wild, lurching circles on the polished tile. "If I had a dress with pockets, I would put my ponies inside!" One arm flailed too wide and she sent a stack of mail spinning over the surface of the desk.

"Do you like ponies?" Belinda asked. Her long-fingered hands skittered over the pockets of her dress like spiders.

Abigail stopped twirling and regarded Belinda solemnly. "You bet. Why, do you have any?"

"Maybe," Belinda said. Her hands ceased their search of the dark folds. "Or maybe I have something better than ponies."

Annie rolled her eyes. Before Abigail could pry into Belinda's cryptic comment any further, the door to the kitchen swung forward and Paul Townsend entered, more dressed up than Annie could ever remember seeing her father look.

"Daddy!" Abbie shouted. "The babysitter has something for us to play with that's better than ponies!"

"You don't say?" He lifted Abigail and planted a kiss on her freckled cheek before setting her down and twirling her like a ballroom dancer. He winked at Annie and checked his watch, then glanced in the direction of his impatient wife. "Are you ready, honey? Sheesh, I've been waiting on you for twenty minutes now." Maggie sighed. Abigail giggled.

"Okay, girls, we have to run or we'll be late for our..."

Annie cocked her head, waiting for her mother to finish, confused by her hesitation.

"Dinner reservation," Paul supplied helpfully.

"Right, our dinner reservation. And after that, a show. And Lord knows your father won't sit through even the best off-Broadway production on an empty stomach. Come kiss us goodbye."

Abigail obliged, but Annie hesitated. *Are they really going out to dinner?*

"Annie," her father said, "come say goodbye to your mother."

Annie trudged across the kitchen and allowed her mother's lotion-perfumed arms to envelope her. When her father leaned down to kiss her forehead, Annie was struck by the impulse to grab onto him and insist that they didn't go, that they send the babysitter home, and that she, Annie, and her parents spend the evening together.

But the moment passed, and her father buttoned his coat

and followed Maggie to the garage. Annie found herself waving at her parents' backs while Abigail shouted her goodbyes.

Belinda and Annie stared at the wall until the rumble of the descending garage door ceased. Belinda turned, her face a blank tableau, before the unseen puppeteer pulled the strings and her mouth hitched up on one side.

"Are you hungry now? Do you want me to heat up the macaroni?"

Abigail made a face. "I'm not hungry for macaroni. I'm hungry for popcorn!"

Belinda looked to Annie as if expecting a protest. When none came, Belinda said, "Suit yourself. Popcorn for dinner it is."

While the foil pocket swelled on the stove, Annie watched Belinda move about the kitchen. She appeared uncomfortable with the implied domesticity of scouring the cabinets for a satisfactory popcorn bowl. When she detected Annie's voyeurism, she gave her that strange half-smile, part teeth, part taut and bloodless lips.

Belinda ushered them into the living room and sat on one end of the sectional, her bony frame sinking into the oversized cushions. Abbie climbed up next to her, and Belinda offered her the near-overflowing bowl of popcorn. Reluctantly, Annie settled in beside her sister. She watched as Abbie plucked a fluffy kernel from the mound and popped it into her mouth.

"Aren't we gonna watch *Moana*?" Abigail asked.

"Sure," Belinda replied. "We can watch your movie. But we have all night. What do you say we get to know each other first? I told you I had something better than ponies to play with, remember?"

Abbie was already nodding, her eyes roving the contours of Belinda's dress, searching for the mysterious offering that was a better prospect than both *Moana* and her vast collection of My Little Ponies; Annie regarded Belinda with suspicion.

"It's not some baby game, is it?" Annie asked, eyes narrowing. "Our last sitter tried to get us to play this game she played when *she* was little, called Pretty Pretty Princess. It was super lame."

"I *liked* Pretty Pretty Princess!" Abbie retorted through a mouthful of popcorn. "And I *liked* Heather too!" Her bow-shaped mouth, shiny with butter, turned down in an exaggerated pout.

"Here," Belinda said, excavating a black-and-crimson fabric bag from her pocket and holding it out to the girls, "open it and see for yourself." She held Annie's eye until Annie looked away. On her left, Abigail had pulled the bag open and was peering inside.

Curious despite herself, Annie leaned closer to her sister. When the light from her mother's reading lamp proved too dim to penetrate its depths, Annie reached over and tipped the bag's contents into Abigail's lap. They marveled at the tiny treasures before them.

Though almost ten, and mature for her age, Annie's proclivity for dolls persisted. Her assortment of Barbies had grown to such proportions that their mother had installed a series of shelves in the bedroom closet as high as Annie was tall to hold all the dolls and their myriad accessories.

Abigail had dolls she enjoyed playing with too, but Abigail's dolls were baby dolls. Annie's dolls were gymnasts practicing for the Olympics, Disney princesses of the more rugged variety, like Pocahontas, and working women with professions like computer engineer and Arctic explorer.

Still, for all her love of tomboys and tough-gals, for the dolls whose clothes could withstand dirt and sand and mud and tears, she harbored a little-girl appreciation for delicate beauty and intricacy of design. And so when the four small dolls had fallen from the drawstring bag and into Abigail's lap, Annie was rendered mute by their exquisiteness.

The dolls were made entirely of fabric, thus the basis for their uniqueness, for that level of detail should have been impossible to achieve with fabric alone. The Mother-doll, for that was how Annie had immediately come to think of her, was dressed in black taffeta, Victorian in style, with lace detail at the wrists and neck like scalloped shells tossed too long at sea.

The cameo around her neck set off expressive emerald eyes.

The male doll was more muted in dress, his dark suit simple but handsome. The two Girl-dolls were done up in deep crimson with ivory accents; one had light brown hair and amber eyes. The other, strawberry blonde hair and green eyes.

The green-eyed girl had a smattering of freckles across her cheeks and nose.

Annie forced her head up, the effort as laborious as if she'd been submerged in a vat of molasses. "Where did you get these?" she asked.

45

"I have always had them," Belinda said.

Abigail, still fingering the dolls lovingly, said without looking up, "They look like us. Like me, and Annie, and Mommy, and Daddy."

Belinda smiled coldly.

Annie felt the room's temperature drop.

"They do look like you and your family, don't they?" Belinda said.

"What are they?" Annie asked.

"Why, they are worry dolls of course. More interesting and well-made worry dolls than most, but still, creatures on which to place your deepest fears and darkest desires all the same." Belinda watched as Annie returned her gaze to her sister's lap; Abbie's had never wavered from there.

"Shall we play with them?"

"Sure," Abbie said, and though Annie felt her sister's enthusiasm was wrong, perverse even, she felt the undeniable urge to agree. She watched as Abigail transported the dolls to the surface of the coffee table, carefully, as if handling an injured bird.

When all four dolls were laid out before them, Belinda leaned forward and said, "You know your parents didn't really go to dinner and to see a show, right Abbie?"

"They didn't?" Abbie asked, in an eerie, toneless voice that Annie thought didn't sound much like her sister. Abigail then took the Mother-doll between thumb and forefinger and stood her on the oak table.

"They didn't," Belinda said. Contrary to the smile Annie had come to expect, Belinda's angular face showed real emotion for the first time since coming in from the rain.

"Where did they go?"

"I will show you," Belinda said.

Annie had not seen Belinda reach back into her pocket; the babysitter produced another drawstring bag with the skill of an illusionist. With a wave of her hand, the new dolls—noticeably dissimilar in appearance from the white-skinned mother doll in traditionally female clothing and the white-skinned father doll in equally traditional masculine garb—rose as if alive, and convened between the walls of a hologram church that materialized with another flick of Belinda's nimble wrist.

"The Mother-doll and Father-doll have gone to a place where love and acceptance reign. But your parents have come for a different purpose."

"No," Annie said hollowly, and felt as though she'd lost some battle she hadn't realized had been waging.

Belinda turned. "Do the Girl-dolls know the doctrines for which their parents campaign?"

Vocabulary was one of Annie's stronger subjects in school, and though she didn't know the exact definition of *doctrine*, she could interpret the meaning of the babysitter's question easily enough. She shook her head.

"I didn't think so."

Abbie yelped as the Mother-doll was pulled from her hand by an unseen force, and moved to join the Father-doll, where they bobbed above the coffee table like a two-headed snake poised to strike. The sisters watched as the eyes of the two dolls changed, first vacillating between black stitched X's and black iridescent pearls, then remaining in their black pearl state so that each doll's face housed a pair of bottomless pits.

Annie felt as if it wouldn't be impossible to fall into one of those pits. The thought was a terrifying one.

The black-eyed Mother-doll approached the church. The holographic light beams were rainbow-patterned, and this drove the Mother-doll to fury. Her stitched doll mouth tore open in a snarl. From beneath the folds of her skirt, she produced a coil of rope and an old-fashioned torch. The tip of the torch burst instantly into flame.

Before Annie could think to ask why, or how, the Father-doll used the rope to tie the doors of the church closed from the outside. The Mother-doll held the blazing torch to the side of the building. The blues, greens, and purples of the rainbow hologram quickly bled away, leaving toxic yellow and molten lava-orange in their wake.

The church began to burn.

The dolls who'd been but superficially different from the white-skinned Mother-and Father-dolls, who'd not been joined in male-female pairings and yet who'd met in acceptance, and in sister-and brotherhood, were still inside.

This isn't real, Annie told herself. It couldn't be. And yet...

Okay, girls, we have to run or we'll be late for our...

Her parents hadn't been trying to make it to any dinner reservation. Annie realized that she'd always known this. The hours her mother spent on the phone, whispering whenever Annie came into the room, the time spent away from home for what were supposed to be parent-teacher conferences, when Annie knew no such meetings had been scheduled, her father's anger and disgust whenever he turned on the news.

Annie's parents had been planning something for some time now. But how could they have orchestrated something such as this?

Annie turned to Abigail and saw that her sister's face had gone very white. "Make it stop," Abigail said. She was fixated on the flames, her small hands balled into fists and shaking. "You're hurting them!"

"You heard her," Annie said. "Put the fire out." She was shaking with fear, but anger, too, pinballed from one organ within her body to the next.

"I can't," Belinda said, feigning surprise. "But I can keep you two from being part of something similar in the future." Belinda lifted the Mother- and Father-doll and turned them toward their children.

"Do you think that if the Daughter-dolls had known what was to happen, they'd have tried to stop it?"

"Yes," Abigail said. She was crying now—almost hyperventilating—and paler still, on the verge of passing out. Annie railed against the evil dolls causing her sister pain; like vampires, they'd drained her tiny form, leaving nothing behind for later. Then she remembered...

The evildoers were not malevolent dolls or supernatural creatures. They were her parents.

"Please," Annie said, feeling helpless.

"If the Daughter-dolls had a choice, would they allow themselves to become ensnared by the Mother and Father's beliefs?"

"No," Annie whispered. Abigail shook her head.

"Then say it," Belinda said. "Say that the Daughter-dolls renounce the doings of their parents."

Annie reached out and clasped Abbie's hand. Silent tears streamed down her own face now.

Abbie's eyes were still glued to the dolls, but Annie felt her little sister's fingers twitch within her own. *She'll be strong if I can find it in myself to be,* Annie thought.

"We want nothing to do with the terrible things Mother and Father have done," Annie said, her voice quiet, but clear. "It's the parents' job to be good. And if they can't be..." She faltered, wiped the tears from her cheeks, and pressed on, "then the Daughter-dolls do not have to be their daughters anymore."

Belinda flicked her wrist. The hologram church disappeared, as did the smoke. The dolls' ruined bodies remained in pieces on the table. The black-eyed Mother-and Father-dolls disappeared into Belinda's pocket.

"Annie, Abbie, get your things. Your mother and father will be home soon, and we have to be gone before they are."

"Can't we wait for them to come back to say goodbye?" Abbie asked.

Annie placed a hand on her sister's arm. "No, Abbie. We can't." She helped Abigail off the couch. "We *will* leave something for them to remember us by," Annie finished, sounding more grownup than she felt.

Belinda smiled her peculiar, partial smile. "Whatever you think is best, my Daughter."

———

Annie struggled to dress Abigail as her mother had always done.

"Don't cry, Abbie. You saw what they did. We have to go with Belinda. It's the only way."

"But why?" Abigail asked miserably. Annie didn't answer. *Stay strong.*

When their bags were packed, Annie clicked off the bedside lamp, plunging the room into darkness. The only illumination came from a sliver of moonlight refracting through an otherwise murky window.

Belinda appeared in the doorway.

"All ready, I see," Belinda said. "That's good." Sirens wailed in the distance. "We have less time than I thought and must be on our way. As Annie said, if parents cannot be relied upon to do right and teach their children the same, then those children have no duty to fulfill their roles as daughters."

Annie regarded Belinda through the darkness. The babysitter pulled something from the folds of her dress.

"Come along, Annie, Abigail. Do not fret. This will be the last night the dark doings of your parents can threaten to stain your souls, a night after which the morning promises to be brighter. You have each other. And you have me. And I'll give you one thing more. Think of it as a shield, if you will. A prayer to ward off evil..." She held out the torch to Annie and with a flick of her wrist, lit its tip.

As Annie led her sister from the only home they'd ever known, touching the licking fire to the curtains, the couch, the coats, as they passed, Belinda recited the verse:

> My kin, their souls were dark and deep,
> They prayed their secrets I would keep.
> And now we've left, daughters no more,
> And pledge to even out the score.

With that, the dark-eyed babysitter beckoned the two sisters forward, to decry dolls and death.

ALL SOULS OF EVE

STAVE ONE
JACK'S DEPARTURE

Eve's ex-boyfriends were dead to begin with.

Three dead exes is a terrible track record, but Evelyn, Eve, Jacobs—twenty-nine years old and still a sucker for a suit and a smile—had terrible taste in men; you will, therefore, permit me to postulate that Frank, Jim, and Adam each succumbing to his respective vice would not come as much of a shock.

Did Eve know how that Ebenezer story went? Of course she did. How could it be otherwise? With everyone from the local theater company to the Muppets doing their part to usher the story into the twenty-first century, she'd seen countless takes on the Ghosts of Christmas Past, Present, and Future.

I mention this because Eve was not only skeptical of the existence of ghosts, she found the prospect of an apparition visiting you with the intention of saving your soul while you were in your nightgown ridiculous. Hell, her grandfather was a real-life Scrooge and Eve would have bet the equivalent of the man's fortune that, if a ghost proposed he share his wealth and promote good cheer or be cast into an early grave, the old man would have knocked the spirit right back out of whatever window it had gained admittance through.

So Eve thought that Dickens' old penny-pincher was a fine morality tale to tell the kiddies, but that there was no more truth to three specters appearing to change the fate of the protagonist than there was to a Jedi Knight, a Wookiee, and a few droids saving the galaxy from an evil empire.

By the time a trio of ghosts had gathered on Eve's balcony to argue over the fate of her soul, Eve would have an entirely different estimation of the supernatural. But alas, I am getting ahead of myself on this All Hallows' Eve, and patience you must have.

Once upon a time—of all the good days in a woman's life, on the night before her wedding—Eve sat busy at her computer desk. She'd finally convinced her mother, an aunt, her best friend, and two cousins to depart for the evening, and only her sister—the maid of honor—remained by her side, looking over Eve's shoulder at a seating chart that had become more convoluted over the last hour, not less.

"What if we put Grandma Irene here?" Cara pointed to an

empty space at a table where their Great-Aunt Louise and several of their mother's work colleagues were already stationed.

Eve squinted, rubbing her temple, and looked up at the younger woman. "Could you please take this home and finish it for me? I can't look at another menu or playlist without my head exploding."

Cara managed to look both sympathetic and put upon. "I haven't been out in town since Michael and I got together. I was planning on hitting the bars for a while, you know, see and be seen?"

Eve dropped her head to the desk and groaned. "You suck," she mumbled through a curtain of hair. "I did everything for you when you and Chris got mar—"

"All right, all right, email it to me and I'll make sure it's done by tomorrow. Nothing like guilting a woman into doing your pre-wedding dirty work by mentioning the unmentionable." Cara sighed. "I don't know why you left everything until the last minute anyway."

Footsteps sounded overhead and Cara turned her gaze to the ceiling. "Who's here?'

Eve inspected the clasp of one of the bracelets around her wrist.

"Don't tell me Jack's upstairs!"

Kneading her forehead with the heel of her hand, Eve still said nothing. The footsteps grew louder and Cara glared at the landing as she waited for her sister's fiancé to appear.

"What's all the goddamn racket?" Jack's mouth twisted into a sneer so slight as to be almost imperceptible, but Eve knew the presence of Cara, hands on hips and ready for combat, was not what Jack wanted to see upon descending the stairs.

"What are you still doing here?" Cara demanded. "You and Eve are supposed to sleep apart the night before the wedding."

"Calm down, I'm getting out of here now. It's early, anyway." He shifted his attention to Eve. "Have you seen my golf clubs?"

"Golf clubs?" Cara's voice rose to a screech. "You're getting married tomorrow, when the hell do you have time to play golf?"

Jack addressed his explanation to his soon-to-be-wife. "The ceremony's not until five, so the guys are taking me in the morning."

Eve let out a deliberately measured breath. "I think they're in the front room of the basement."

"Great." He made as if to head that way, then turned back. "What about that gift card for the Winnapaug course? Seen that lying around?"

Eve closed her eyes in thought. "Kitchen desk, middle drawer on the left."

Jack hurried from the room, ignoring Cara's pointed stare. When he'd gone, Cara said, "Are you sure you don't want to come out for a bit? Or at least have me and Michael come back here to keep you company? Just because Jack's not supposed to be with you doesn't mean you have to be alone."

Eve pushed back from the desk and yawned. "I'll be fine, Car, really. I'm going to pour some vino, take a bath, and hopefully get enough sleep for these circles under my eyes to disappear."

Cara's skepticism was written in the tilt of her head, the discerning expression on her face.

I want to be alone, Eve thought, surprised by the anger that had bloomed within her. *Why is that so hard to understand?*

"Okay," Cara said, still sounding uncertain. She collected her purse and jacket from the couch, and peered out the window into the waning sunlight. "Make sure Jack doesn't stay much longer. And I'll finish the damn seating chart, so don't worry about that."

"Thank you. Have fun tonight. And don't go too crazy. You've got a wedding to be in tomorrow." Eve wrapped her sister in a hug.

She saw Cara out and sank onto the couch. Still rubbing her pounding head, Eve had decided to skip the wine when Jack appeared in the doorway. "You find the gift card?"

When Jack didn't answer, Eve looked up.

He was red-faced, practically vibrating with rage. He held a piece of paper in one hand, and forced a rueful, sarcastic chuckle Eve didn't like the sound of.

"What's that?" Even as she asked the question, Eve realized what Jack held, what he'd found in the left-hand drawer of the kitchen, right where she'd directed him. *How could I have forgotten that was in there?*

"Do you want to attempt to explain this? Or can we cut the shit and move right to the part where I call you a liar?"

"Hey!" Eve exclaimed, but she was stalling for time.

"Hey, what? *Hey, you caught me*, or *hey, just kidding, Jack, even though we agreed we weren't in a position for me to quit my fucking job and fuck around as a graphic designer without a single client signed up, I went ahead and copyrighted my stupid company name anyway?"*

"Don't be ridiculous, I didn't quit my job. I was playing around."

"Playing around, huh?" Jack took three long strides and shoved the paper in her face. "You paid sixty-five dollars for a copyright license. Tell me how that's playing around."

Indignation caused Eve's cheeks to flush, but she felt panicky, too, that Jack was really upset with her, despite her benevolent intentions. "It's sixty-five dollars. I don't think it's going to break us.'

"Coupled with the cost of this fucking wedding, it might."

Eve jumped to her feet and stalked across the room toward the bar. She took a bottle of red from beneath the cabinet, slid a long-stemmed glass from the rack above, and poured herself a generous serving. She pointed the bottle in Jack's direction and raised an eyebrow in offering.

He scoffed. "Enter Mrs. Fix-it. Always trying to smooth things over."

"How terrible of me to want things to be smoothed over between us the night before our wedding." She swigged from her glass.

"You only want things smoothed over because you're the one who fucked them up. We talked about this. How will we be able to start a family if you're working for yourself? That's if you've even done well enough to have amassed any clients. You haven't done that type of design work since right after college, when you were dating that chain-smoking loser of a deejay. You can't—"

Jack stopped abruptly and shook his head in disgust. "I'm not doing this right now. As your ever-helpful slut of a sister pointed out, we're not even supposed to be under the same roof tonight. I wonder if she and Chris abided by that rule, or if she's planning on doing better with Michael this time around."

He slipped into his coat and patted his pocket for his keys. "I'll be at Clayton's tonight, and on the golf course in the morning. Only call if you really need something. I think we could use the time apart tonight."

Eve felt a storm system move into her stomach and begin to churn.

He'll realize he's overreacting before he leaves and tell me that he loves me. He'll tell me we're going to make this marriage work, that the graphic design company has potential, and that he doesn't want to spend the night before our wedding upset with one another.

Jack brushed past her, slipped outside without looking back, and slammed the door.

Eve sat motionless on the couch for half an hour. When she was certain Jack would not be returning—that no apology was forthcoming—and with nothing else to do but carry on as if a lamentable but not entirely unexpected fight had *not* occurred the evening before their nuptials, she went upstairs to draw a bath.

She swiped the remote from Jack's side of the bed so she could flip through the channels while the tub filled. A movie was beginning; the guide identified it as *All Hallows' Eve*.

"Damn," she said, remembering the holiday for the first time in hours.

She ran back downstairs, set the candy out on the porch, and returned to the bedroom to immerse herself in the plot of a murderous clown, a VHS tape, and an unsuspecting babysitter on Halloween night.

STAVE TWO
THE FIRST OF THE THREE SPIRITS

By the time Eve peeled her eyes from the on-screen bloodbath, the water in the tub had gone cold. She drained two thirds of it, set the tap to scalding, and refilled her wine glass from the bottle on the floor. She then returned to her spot on the bed to witness the babysitter's fate.

The film ended as the water hit the emergency drain. Eve let the robe puddle around her feet, slid into the tub, and closed her eyes. As the heat eased the tension from her muscles, her mind drifted from psychopathic clowns to floral centerpieces, then blended the two, horror film melding with impending matrimony; mutilated bridesmaids ran from reception halls filling with blood, as if an elevator in The Overlook Hotel had opened onto the room.

She smiled at the macabre slideshow her harried brain had produced.

"You know," came a voice from the edge of the tub, "you were always so pretty when you smiled."

Eve's eyes flew open and she beheld Frank Quattrochi,

ex-boyfriend from another life. *Dead* ex-boyfriend from another life. Eve yelped and pulled her knees to her chest, causing a small tidal wave to slosh over the side of the claw foot tub.

"What the—? How are you—?" Eve looked to her half-drunk third glass of wine, and wondered if the mixture of stress, alcohol, and heat was causing her to hallucinate.

Frank smiled. "Don't be afraid."

"Why are you here?"

Frank shrugged. "It's All Hallows' Eve. I'm here because I can be. The boundary between the physical and spiritual worlds is thin, so I've come to see you before you embark on the darker half of the year. And, incidentally, on your marriage."

Eve relaxed slightly. *I'm speaking with someone I shouldn't have ever been able to speak with again.* She noticed that the water she'd displaced had gone *through* Frank to the floor below, and quickly looked away.

"Can you hand me that towel and robe?"

He held them out to her. Eve contemplated getting into the robe wet then figured that not only had Frank seen her naked before, he was also, somehow, a ghost and had likely witnessed her getting *into* the bath.

She dried off and followed Frank out of the bathroom. There was a balcony off the master bedroom, and this was where Frank steered her now. She stood next to him by the railing and watched in amazement as he took a pack of cigarettes from his pocket and lit one.

"You didn't get enough of those on your suicide mission here on Earth?"

Frank shrugged again. "No point in *not* smoking now." He looked to the street below. "How's life?"

"How's life?" Eve laughed. "You come back from the dead after ten years and all you can ask is, *how's life?*"

Frank's dark eyes crinkled. "How's this, then? Do you miss me?"

That was a more interesting question. "I'm not sure."

"You loved me once, right?"

Eve bit the inside of her cheek. "Once, yes. That was a long time ago though."

Frank looked at her as if no time had passed at all. He held out his hand. "Let me refresh your memory."

Despite her trepidation, Eve lifted her hand from the rail, and reached for Frank's.

As their fingers intertwined, the moonlit balcony blurred. A moment later, it winked from existence. When Eve's vision refocused, she was standing in the doorway of a darkened room. She turned, found Frank still beside her.

Before them in a small, equipment-clogged deejay booth, a younger Eve, dressed in a red satin corset, black booty shorts, and fishnet stockings, faced a version of Frank not much different from the one still holding her hand.

"It's... us. It's the night we first met." Eve paused. "What was I thinking with that outfit?"

Frank smiled, put a finger to his lips, and nodded toward the people they'd once been.

The other Frank's hands flew over the keyboard as he searched for whatever song the next dancer had requested. A ring bedecked each finger, and he wore his thick black hair in a pompadour and sideburns, a Marlboro tucked behind one ear.

The younger Eve looked lost. "Rather than introduce me to people, the manager told me to *wander* until I'd met everyone. So, yeah, I'm Eve, the new cocktail waitress."

The former Frank's grin affected his entire face. Dimples appeared in both cheeks, his brows lifted into pleasant V's, and smile lines bracketed dark brown eyes. "Nice to meet you, Eve. I'm Frank. How long are you going to make me grovel before you agree to be my girlfriend."

Eve laughed. "Right. Has there ever been a new girl you *didn't* try that line on?"

Before Frank could respond, a shimmery-skinned dancer in a purple foil bikini and eight-inch thigh-high pleather books slunk past Eve and into the booth.

"You get my set ready, Frankie?" she purred.

Frank gestured toward the screen. "You bet. I even found the extended version of that Ciara song you like."

"You're the best." The dancer leaned onto the toes of her boots to kiss Frank on the cheek.

"Diamond, do me a favor will you? Tell Eve here how many women from the Crazy Horse I've dated."

Diamond arranged her glossed lips in a pout. "Why're you teasing me, Frankie baby?" She turned to Eve. "I've worked here four years and Frank's been torturing me and every other dancer, waitress, and bartender in the joint for that same amount of time."

Realizing why Frank had requested her input, Diamond scowled and looked Eve up and down. "If Frank's going to ask out someone from the club, then my own mother really and truly named me Diamond Skye."

"You're on in thirty seconds," Frank called after her as she sidled from the room. He grinned at Eve. "Now do you believe me? So, when're you going to let me take you out?"

The scene dissipated like a reflection in a disturbed pool of water. Eve and Frank stood on Philadelphia's South 5th Street in a growing layer of snow. More snow fell from the sky, thick, wet flakes that blanketed the brick-sided townhouses and caught in Eve's eyelashes.

"How long was it that you made me wait?"

"It wasn't *that* long, and you can't blame me for being wary. I only got that job after graduation to delay deciding between filling out marketing applications or pursuing my own design company. I was out of my element at a gentlemen's club."

"It was over a month," Frank reminded her. He looked up at the window of a two-story townhouse. "But after that, we were together nonstop. It wasn't long before you moved in here with me."

Eve stepped over to stand beside Frank and followed his gaze to the window. In an instant, they were transported to the room from which the window looked out.

The earlier rendition of Frank had a white sheet wrapped around his torso, a scarf cinching it closed, and was serenading the younger Eve with a number from *Jesus Christ Superstar*.

Eve looked at Frank's ghost by her side and smiled sadly. "You always loved your music. All kinds, too. It's why your deejay company was so successful."

"The company was successful because of you."

She said nothing in response, remembering how many

hours she'd spent designing the logo for Frankie's Flimflam Fusion Entertainment, and how little time she'd started putting into her own designs. Eve looked back to the couple in the living room, watched as Frank tackled her onto a worn leather couch and kissed her, wrapping the scarf around her neck, pulling her close.

"We had a lot of fun here," she admitted.

The scene before them flickered and the positions of the players changed. Eve sat at a small desk in the corner, completing a task for the corporate marketing giant that had hired her the month before. Frank watched television from the couch, a cigarette in his mouth, a near-overflowing ashtray balanced on his chest. The telephone rang.

"That was my uncle calling," ghost-Frank said to her. "Do you remember that day?"

Tears stung Eve's eyes. "Of course."

As if her words had summoned the vision, Eve stood next to Frank on the outskirts of a funeral sermon. The former Frank was closest to the open grave, leaning against Eve, his eyes red, a pack of cigarettes visible in the breast pocket of his black suit.

Frank turned to Eve. "This was the end for my father. But it was the beginning of the end for us too."

"You say that like it's my fault," Eve said. "You were crushed when your father died, but I supported you as much as possible. I couldn't change your cigarette consumption— up to three packs a day by then—or your father's death exacerbating your mother's mental health issues."

"No, but you could have reacted differently to the job offer in LA."

"I didn't end up taking it," Eve protested bitterly.

"But you interviewed for it. Made me think you were going to abandon me during the worst time of my life."

"I asked you to come with me."

"Knowing I couldn't leave my business."

They stared at one another, at the same impasse they'd come to ten years earlier.

"You gave me that awful letter." Eve gripped Frank's arm, forced him to look her in the eye. "Are you going to show me that night?"

Frank shrugged, took her hand, and they were standing on the street again, overlooking a van with Eve's design for Frankie's Flimflam Fusion screen-printed across the side. Frank was in the front seat, window down, exhaling large puffs of cigarette smoke. The Eve in the passenger seat had a creased and tear-stained letter in her hands.

"How could you write this?" Eve asked, gripping the letter so hard her nails tore holes through the page. "Do you really think I'm not ready to run a graphics department? That my work has gotten worse over the past few months, not better?"

The bygone version of Frank lit a new cigarette with the dying embers of the old one. "I'm sorry if it seemed harsh, but I don't think the company that hired you knows what they're doing. It's stupid to uproot your life for a place willing to hire someone so green. Here, you can focus on the things you've been wanting to improve, without having to worry about being in a new city, without friends or family, and, well, without me."

"You were so manipulative," Eve whispered to ghost-

Frank. "You broke me down. You made me think I was nothing without you, and in turn that made me think I was nothing at all." Eve looked away from the van. Up the road, a street light buzzed off, then on again, before going out.

"Take me home, Frank. We know what happens next. I stay and things are never the same. We break up. You kill yourself with a cocktail of nicotine and carcinogens, because not only was I not worth quitting for, but neither were you."

Frank sighed, beholding the former Frank convincing the former Eve she wasn't good enough at the very thing she wanted to succeed at most, and took her hand. Eve closed her eyes.

When she opened them, they were standing on her upstairs balcony once more. A gaggle of costumed girls, including an undead snow queen and dolled-up comic supervillain, sprinted off a neighbor's porch. Laughter and shouts of *trick-or-treat* reached her ears from farther down the street.

Eve watched Frank stamp out a cigarette and kick it over the railing to the leaf-choked gutter below.

"Why are you really here?" she pressed. "I know it's not because you can be, or because you wanted to remind me of our past together. So, why?"

Frank lit another cigarette, the lighter illuminating his face in the dark.

"It's All Hallows' Eve... and my soul needs propitiation."

Eve's skin prickled. "Your soul needs to be propitiated. Right. And how am I supposed to help you with that?"

"You can spend this All Hallows' Eve with me," he gave her a suggestive wink, "like we used to, remember?"

Eve ignored the wink, and its connotations. "Or?"

"Or, offer up a portion of your soul on a future Halloween. The first upon your death."

"What's behind door number three?"

Frank looked surprised. "Option three is you condemn my spirit to roam the earth until the All Hallows' Eve on which I *am* propitiated. But Eve," he said, and she remembered that expectant tone well, "I need you to do this for me."

"You do, huh? You want me to either lay with the ghost of my ex-lover the night before my wedding, or make a deal with the Devil and give up a *portion* of my soul upon my death? Then what? I suppose, if I agree to that, I'm sentenced to the same fate, wandering between the spirit world and the physical one until someone agrees to do the same for me?"

Frank's face lit up like a boy offered king-sized candy bars as trick-or-treat loot. "Exactly! You have until midnight to make your decision. Don't be hasty, Eve. Please."

And with that, he disappeared, leaving behind the faint scent of cigarette smoke in the crisp autumn air.

STAVE THREE
THE SECOND OF THE THREE SPIRITS

Eve pulled her robe tighter and turned to go inside.

What time is it? How long do I have until Frank comes back to hear my decision?

Eve thought again of the terms. Her relationship with Jack was rocky, but did that mean she'd be willing to have a one-night stand with a ghost? The idea was ridiculous. But what about the second option? Did she care enough about an old boyfriend to spend the first part of her afterlife an aimless wanderer of purgatory?

"This is crazy."

"But you like crazy, don't you? I mean, you must, otherwise you wouldn't have spent so much time with me."

Eve knew Paul Abello's voice before looking up. He stood in the doorway of the balcony, his sandy-colored hair still thick and long, his eyes indeed as wild as ever.

"Paul," she said, and could find no other words.

"Yes, my love."

"Do we have to go back? I'm not sure I can bear to see it all again."

"I'm sorry, my love." He approached her slowly, one hand extended toward hers. "There were things that were difficult, I won't deny that. But there were good times too. I want to show you those."

She felt the surprising warmth of Paul's hand. A thick mist blew in from the west. It rolled over the balcony and consumed them. When it cleared, she was peering through the window of a coffee shop in South Boston at her and Paul's first date.

"I forgot about this day," Eve said dazedly. "I'd moved to Southie the week before. After everything that happened, I forgot about the lies at the foundation of our relationship."

"They weren't lies." Paul crossed arms covered in black-ink tattoos. "They just weren't true at that exact moment."

Eve whipped around to protest, but Paul shook his head and pointed. Eve could hear the conversation as if the glass had been a screen.

"What do you do, Paul?" Eve asked. Paul sipped an iced coffee and gave her a lazy grin. "I've been with Safety Insurance for years. My dad worked there his whole career, so he's pretty stoked I'm following in his footsteps. I'm getting a few buddies in the door there too. It's great, number three insurance company in all of Beantown."

Eve turned to Paul's ghost, unable to help herself. "Let's see if I remember the status of those lies-that-weren't-true-at-that-exact-moment. Safety fired you months prior, your parents wanted nothing to do with you, and your buddies were the other recovering addicts and alcoholics who lived in the halfway house a few blocks away. Do I have that right?"

Ghost-Paul's response was drowned out by laughter from inside the coffee shop, and Eve spun to regard her former self amused by something Paul had said. He returned her question, and she listened to a younger, more naïve Eve discuss her attempts at getting the graphic design company off the ground.

"How is the company?" ghost-Paul asked.

Eve inspected the clasp of her bracelet. "It's fine. Great, really. Was there somewhere else you wanted to show me?"

Paul took her hand. A red-rock quarry buttressing an expansive apartment complex replaced the coffee shop. They made their way through the lobby and down a well-lit hall to a unit at the back of the building.

"I remember living here like it was yesterday," Eve said.

"It was a great complex."

Eve stopped walking, forcing Paul to turn and look at her. "It was also the backdrop for one too many traumatic incidents. The brain translates short-term details into long-term memory when either extreme pleasure or extreme distress is experienced."

Paul fixed her with that *are you done yet?* look she despised so much and then continued down the hallway. The first thing Eve spotted inside the old apartment was the glow of the television across the room. A History Channel documentary on the lore and legend of Halloween played at low volume. Eve leaned against the wall, feeling ill.

"I remember this night."

A gaunt and sickly-looking Paul lay on the blanket-strewn couch, ignoring the documentary for the paraphernalia on the coffee table before him. He stirred a spoonful of dark brown liquid with the plunger rod of a syringe, flipped it, and drew the mixture up until the chamber was completely full.

Eve's breath hitched as she watched Paul tie off and injected 100 CCs of china white heroin into a recently-detoxed vein. His face contorted in a mask of euphoria and he fell to his side on the couch. Paul's breathing slowed, but a wheezing, agitated gasp escaped his lungs; it was this that brought a sleep-disoriented Eve from the bedroom.

After calling his name and receiving no response, Eve crept toward the couch. She shook Paul's shoulder. A corner of the blanket came untucked, and the empty syringe fell into view.

"I still have never been more shocked by anything in my entire life," the present Eve said. "I mean, I knew you'd relapsed. That's why you moved in with me far earlier than was healthy for any new relationship. But I believed you when you said it'd been a stupid mistake, that you loved me enough that it wouldn't happen again."

She turned back to the memory, watched a panicked version of herself scream at a 911 operator and perform CPR.

"You were lucky that night," Eve said flatly. "But you weren't lucky after I made you go back into treatment. I'd changed the locks. You overdosed then, like it was my fault."

Sirens sounded in the distance. Eve turned away from her attempts to revive Paul. "Can we get out of here?" She grasped the ghost's hand without waiting for a reply.

Her own balcony took shape, and she suppressed the desire to drop to her knees and lay her cheek upon the wood, emotionally drained.

I have a newfound sympathy for Ebenezer Scrooge.

She turned on Paul, anger clawing at her like a thousand syringe tips at fragile skin. "I blamed myself," she said. "I never forgave myself for not giving you another chance. I went over the day you died a thousand times in my head. I'd saved you once, what if I'd been able to save you again? What if letting you come home would have kept you from relapsing again?

"I thought I was giving you a dose of tough love, but all I did was condemn myself to months of agony. I couldn't sleep. All the work I'd done on my company fell by the wayside. Guilt made grief impossible to get over."

She looked at his handsome face and capable hands, hands that'd drafted thousands of insurance policies, distributed dozens of sobriety medallions to newcomers in AA, caressed her body innumerable times.

"You broke me, and it took so goddamn long to put myself back together again. Have you really come to ask for something more?"

If Paul faltered, Eve saw no sign of it. His features maintained their lazy, boyish repose. "You said yourself, what if? What if you'd done things differently? What if you'd been able to save me again? Well, now you can."

Paul floated forward and embraced her.

"At the very least," he whispered. "We could be together again, if only for the night."

Eve pulled away, chastising herself for the re-ignited feelings of guilt that surfaced when she did. "I don't think so."

His face fell as it had when she'd refused him money or a ride to score drugs. She knew what came next and held up her hand before he could begin.

"Begging won't work. I haven't determined how I feel about sharing my soul. My guess would be I have until midnight to make that decision?"

"Yes." He lifted a hand to stroke her face.

Cool air fanned her cheek.

"I've always loved you," he said, as his form began to flicker.

"Perhaps," Eve said as he disappeared, "but love wasn't enough."

STAVE FOUR
THE LAST OF THE SPIRITS

Eve came in off the balcony and stood, dreading the moment the clock would strike twelve.

Scrooge was visited by three spirits, she thought, exhausted. *At least I only have two dead ex-boyfriends.*

On the television, the doorbell rang. The station that had played *All Hallows' Eve* was showing the film back-to-back, and the hapless babysitter was being menaced by that barbaric clown all over again. The doorbell clanged a second time, and then a third, before Eve realized it was *her* doorbell that was ringing, and headed for the stairs.

She snagged the bag of bite-sized chocolate from the counter, figuring the cache on the porch had run dry. The doorbell rang again. "For Samhain's sake, I'm fucking coming," she muttered.

She flung open the door, prepared to teach the Zombie-Elsa and Harley Quinn she'd seen earlier a thing or two about trick-or-treating etiquette.

Adam Barclay stood beneath her porch light, skin flickering.

Adam can't be dead, Eve thought wildly. *He was posting on Facebook this morning.*

"So you haven't heard," the ghost said, in response to her shocked expression. "I suppose my family will keep it under wraps a few more days, before the obituary is in the paper."

Eve continued to stare.

"I killed myself early this morning. I did it because I couldn't have you."

Anger mobilized her into speech. "What? Because of me? Are you kidding me?"

"I'm not kidding." Adam's chiseled visage scrunched into a pout. "Why would I joke about something like that?"

"It's just that... I pursued you for over a year! I mean, I pursued you even while we were *together*. Even when you were with me, you weren't really with me. You cheated and came crawling back, over and over again. You messed with my head for months, got me so I couldn't succeed at picking off nail polish let alone my work. Eventually, I smartened up, moved on. Three years later, you're telling me *I'm* the reason you—?" An exasperated cry escaped Eve's lips.

Adam... the red herring in my co-dependency recovery. At least, that's what my therapist said.

Adam's pout became an offended grimace.

"I saw on social media you were getting married tomorrow. I couldn't deal. I've been so alone since we split."

"You mean since I caught you cheating with Mandy, or Candy, or whatever the hell her name was?"

"You're not listening! Look, I'm sorry for the shit I did when we were together. I was scared of having such a strong woman like you and—"

"Save it, Adam." She turned and started for the stairs. Adam followed. "Let me guess," she continued, "you're *so* scared, you need me to be with you for one more night, or sacrifice my peace in the afterlife to help you?"

Eve could see that Adam was going to agree with her before he opened his mouth. *Why wouldn't he? Of course that's what he's after; it's what they're all after.*

As they entered her bedroom, Adam's reply was lost to a scream emanating from the television. That damn clown was hacking off the girl's limbs for the fourth time tonight.

Fuck this horror film, Eve thought. *Fuck all horror films. The final girl may live, but she's stripped of so much by the time the credits roll.*

The knowledge of Adam's suicide blared in her head like a too-loud announcement in a department store. That he claimed she was the cause was maddening beyond comprehension. She was not responsible for Adam's loneliness; similarly, she was not responsible for Frank's happiness, or Paul's recovery.

Ja-cob MARLEY, Eve thought in amazement. They *weren't responsible for* my *success or fulfillment either.*

Eve looked at the clock on the nightstand. It was almost midnight.

"I'm upset to hear that you've taken your own life," Eve said. "But I'm going to shut the door now. I'll see you with the others momentarily."

"The others?" Adam's voice was a pathetic whimper, but he stepped over the threshold and onto the balcony.

Eve flung the slider shut, and pulled the curtain across the glass.

STAVE FIVE

THE END OF IT

On the television, the telephone rang. A moment later, the phone on her nightstand did the same.

"Jesus," Eve said. "I really wish that would stop happening."

She considered letting it ring, then wondered how she'd explain three dead ex-boyfriends on her balcony if it was her sister calling to say she and Michael were coming to Eve's place after all. She sprang for the phone. "Hello?"

"Yeah, it's me." Jack's tone left little doubt as to his lingering anger. "Listen, I can't talk. I'm just calling to tell you that I'm at Clayton's, and Greg and Jeff are here. Jeff was telling me about a few friends that are looking for a graphic designer. He said they're willing to pay upwards of a hundred bucks an hour, so I told him for *that* kind of money—"

Eve placed the phone down on the bed. *I allowed each of them to take so much from me, and did nothing to raise myself up in return. If I marry Jack tomorrow, it will be like throwing myself under the murderous clown's hacksaw. Like pitching a tent on the banks of Crystal Lake. I'll only have myself to blame...*

Eve peeked around the edge of the curtain. The three spirits had convened. She hurried to the closet, pushed her wedding dress to one side, and felt around until her fingers brushed a coarse swatch of fabric.

Before they'd picked a date for the wedding, Jack had wanted to go out for Halloween as Star Wars characters. Eve had ordered Rey and Finn costumes off the internet; Jack had sneered when they'd arrived.

"*The Force Awakens* is not *Star Wars*," he'd said. "I meant original *Star Wars*, like Han and Leia *Star Wars*. You think I'd go as the pussy sidekick to your chick character?"

Eve dressed quickly, pulling the wraparound scarf around her head and chest, and lowering the eye mask. She left the curtain closed and the movie on, stole across the room and down the stairs.

As she crossed the yard beneath a cover of fog, she heard a commotion from above.

"Is that her?" Paul asked. "It's midnight now."

"That's not her," Frank said. "That woman's dressed for Halloween."

As evasive as Rey escaping her assailants on Jakku, Eve slunk down the street. Let the spirits of those from her past wander and want for, as she had. Tomorrow, Jack could wander around the altar looking for her, too.

From now on, I survive the final act on the basis of my own abilities. The only one responsible for my successes or failures is me. That's a promise.

When Eve had turned the corner, heading in the direction of the downtown bars, Frank took a cigarette from his pocket, lit it, and said, "Did the ghosts in Dicken's tale get to revel in the knowledge of their success?"

"I'm not sure," Paul replied, "but earning propitiation was even sweeter, knowing we did our part to make her happy."

Adam smirked. "I still think if she'd chosen anyone, it would have been me."

Frank, Paul, and Adam's auras flickered, and in the moment before they disappeared, they smiled, for they knew, though she would have no further interactions with Spirits, that as far as honoring her promise to keep Halloween by subverting the very *final girl* tropes she so despised, Eve would be better than her word.

LIQUID HANDCUFFS

Nicole Price spun into the office like a tornado having amassed substantial debris and flopped onto the threadbare fabric chair the same way she did every week: heavily-mascaraed, sweatpants-clad, and reeking of cigarette smoke. Her long black hair was strung through an elastic band in a gravity-defying poof, and the coiffure surged and crested in the squalls of her third-generation-Italian-induced hand gestures.

"Oh... my... God," she said by way of starting the session, tarantula-leg lashes batting up and down as her eyes moved over the screen of her cell phone, "I have so much to tell you."

Condensation dripped from the large iced coffee in her hand, and she paused to drink from it. The Sharpie scribbling on the side of the cup identified the beverage as *Xtra lite/ Xtra sweet,* and Nicole visibly crunched on a mouthful of sugar.

She placed the still sweating cup on the floor by her feet—Ugg boots, though it was well into June—and focused her attention on the woman sitting across from her for the first time since entering the room.

Olive Holton crossed her legs at the ankles and fingered the pearl necklace dangling above the collar of her silk blouse. She smiled indulgently and raised an eyebrow, indicating she was ready for Nicole to begin.

"Did you know that Dunkin Donuts' straws are the *exact* same shade of orange as the syringes from the Rite Aid down the street?" The expression on Nicole's face suggested she was envisioning the less benign of these items. "When I told my last counselor this, she said I shouldn't go to Dunks anymore because it could—and I quote—*trigger me to use.*" She rolled her eyes.

"I was like, *what are you, stupid? I go to Dunks every morning before I get my dose, and every afternoon before my shift. Come up with a new coping skill, or relapse prevention plan, or whatever other psycho-babble-bullshit you want, but do not threaten my caffeine fix.* She didn't appreciate that too much, but I mean, what the fuck!" Nicole thrust her hands out in a coinciding *what the fuck?* gesture. Droplets of water flew from the side of the cup and splattered on the floor.

Olive nodded thoughtfully. "You were still using when you were working with your last counselor. It sounds like she had ample cause with which to make her suggestion, no?" The question was confrontational, but Olive's tone was kind.

Olive had established a strong enough rapport with Nicole to know that her patient would respond agreeably to this tactic.

Nicole pawed at the air as if she were slapping Olive on the back. "You got me there. But that's why I like you." She grinned. "You call me on my shit."

Olive gave a noncommittal wave of her hand; Nicole's gesticulations were sometimes catching. "I'm not calling you on anything, just looking at things from a different angle. You might be able to fake a drug screen once or twice, but you can't fake your whole recovery. You're doing very well now, anyone can see that."

Olive watched Nicole to register how she would take the praise. She tried to be direct with her patients, to avoid both clichés and academic jargon. To date, she had never told a patient she was going to *administer* a series of cognitive behavioral therapy questions to uncover automatic thoughts, but sometimes she worried she was too informal with them or laid on the positive reinforcement too thickly.

Olive's worst fear was that she would engage in some type of behavior a patient could perceive as indicative of the differences between her, the counselor, and them, the patient. The clinic's treatment module already stipulated the use of the word *patient* over *client*, a lesson in semantics Olive was less than thrilled with. She supposed *patient* was better than *addict*, and was sure those less sympathetic to the disease of addiction (or those convinced addiction wasn't even a disease) could come up with worse. It was why she'd framed a print declaring *Appearances can be deceiving* and hung it on her office wall. In short, Olive did not want unconditional positive regard to come across as condescension.

In Nicole's case, she needn't have worried.

"I soooo appreciate you being real with me. It's crazy how understanding you are of everything: the lifestyle, the cravings, having to abandon old friends, how hard it is sometimes. All the shit that comes with getting clean." Nicole paused, worrying a large obsidian ring on her middle finger. Even in moments of quiet, the girl's hands were always moving.

"It's almost like you've been through it."

Olive shifted in her chair.

Nicole continued, "Everyone says you're the most understanding counselor here, and I'm glad I got you."

Olive let her gaze rove, and found a small piece of plastic on the scratched-up surface of her desk. It looked like the bottom corner of a sandwich baggie, but was likely a byproduct of the new package of appointment cards Olive had torn into that morning. Olive stared at it, transfixed by its presence there. She watched as it quivered in the wake of her exhalation.

"You all right?" Nicole asked.

"Hmm? Oh. Yes, of course, I was just thinking. West Street Neighborhood Health Center is the first facility I've worked at that had a non-disclosure policy. I agree that it's odd. I would think the doctors that own this network of clinics would want to reduce stigma and promote good recovery role models for their patients, but I don't make the rules. I *do* try my best to be understanding." She gave Nicole a pointed look. "I *do* understand."

Olive steered the session in a new direction. "How's your

mother doing?"

"Eh, the same, more or less. I tried to convince her to hire a cleaning service to go over once a week, you know, to help her out some, since she's basically living in squalor. She should be using her disability for food and clothes and other essentials, but she spends all her money on drugs, so a cleaning lady would be a step up. Anyone else would have lost their housing by now, but, well, you know the deal. The state won't evict someone who's HIV positive, and my mom thinks her diagnosis is an excuse to keep up the self-regulated opioid cocktail in lieu of her Retrovir."

Olive pursed her lips. Nicole's mother had been a patient at West Street for several months before she'd been kicked off for non-compliance. "I'm sorry to hear that. That you've managed to stabilize on your dose enough to stop using, while still living with your mom, it shows how committed you are to your recovery."

Nicole shot her a conspiratorial look. "That's what I couldn't wait to tell you. I'm not going to have to deal with it anymore."

"What do you mean?"

"I got my own place! It's a one-bedroom on Revere Beach, with a parking spot and laundry in unit, and it's absolutely perfect."

"That's great news! How did you find the apartment?"

"You know Jill, that bartender I've mentioned before? She's on during my weekend shifts? Her boyfriend, Andy, has a unit in the same building and is tight with the building manager. Andy talked him into waiving last month's rent and a security deposit, so all I needed to come up with was the initial grand. He told him I had a solid job and wouldn't be an issue in terms of paying, and the manager agreed to it. I *knew* hooking Jill up at tip-out night after night would pay off!"

"Do you have pictures?"

Nicole slid her chair forward to scroll through an album highlighting the apartment's amenities. The unit was clean and bright, and Revere Beach was right across the street from the complex's front door.

Many of Olive's patients lived on or around Revere Beach. Olive hadn't understood how waterfront property could be so cheap prior to an explanation from her six o'clock patient, Eugene Salvestri: "Revere Beach? You mean Needle Beach?"

Nicole scooted her chair back and beamed at Olive. "I told you. It's perfect, right?"

"It really is. The fact that you have guaranteed parking is key. I know you hated searching for street parking when you got out of work late, especially when you had to pick up Eddie from whatever chaos he was engaged in. Speaking of Eddie, how's he taking all of this?" Olive struggled to keep her tone neutral.

Eddie Vance. The most abrasive, manipulative patient on the clinic and Nicole's long-time boyfriend up until two weeks ago, the chip on Eddie's shoulder was as large as the fuse on his temper was short. Eddie had probably been good-looking once, but years of hard living and harder drugging had given his features a pinched look that somehow grew more severe when he smiled. Fortunately, this brand of facial expression was a rarity.

Nicole sighed and threw up her hands. "You know him. I'm not giving in this time. I thought there was a chance I was getting the apartment when I broke up with him a few weeks ago and purposely said nothing. Not only am I not speaking to him, I'm not even telling him I moved. He'll find out soon enough, I'm sure. I'm surprised he hasn't gotten one of his derelict friends to drive him to my mom's looking for me already."

Nicole wrung her hands. Her words were confident but it was obvious that severing her ties to Eddie had been rough. During a session two weeks ago, when she'd divulged to Olive that she'd ended things with Eddie, Nicole had teared up despite her best efforts to keep her carefully-coated lashes intact.

"How do you think he'll react when he finds out you have your own place?"

Nicole gave her a wide-eyed look of horror. "Um, terribly. He's going to go into full manipulation mode, try to talk me into taking him back. You know how often he stayed with me at my mom's; it was like five or six nights a week. Maybe more. It'll kill him to know I finally have my own place and he can't reap the benefits."

"You don't think he'd do anything dangerous, do you?" Olive asked.

Eddie had been spoken to by staff several times, warning him to keep his distance from the other patients and reminding him of the clinic's no-tolerance policy for threatening behavior. Eddie had taken to whistling at Nicole when he passed her in line for his dose, and sneering at Olive when she came into the lobby to collect her patients for session. He was convinced that Olive was responsible for Nicole breaking up with him and blamed her for the subsequent drying up of his transportation, living situation, and singular money source.

Nicole frowned while she fiddled with her hair. "Eddie talks a lot of shit but that's all it is. He showed up at Giacomo's two nights ago demanding to see me, and Bobby had to kick him out. He told Eddie not to show his face in the North End again or he'd beat his ass."

"I don't think showing up at your place of employment constitutes mere *talk*," Olive said. "Can you have someone walk with you to your car at the end of your shift?"

"Bobby has one of the bussers or dishwashers walk the girls out every night. I'm not worried. Eddie's way too much of a pussy to stand up to Bobby; after Bobby told him to kick rocks, Eddie slunk away with his tail between his legs. Don't get me wrong, I wouldn't be surprised if Eddie does *something* to salvage his wounded pride. But it'll be petty and childish, like egging Bobby's car or prank calling the restaurant."

"Where were you when Bobby was kicking him out?"

"Jill saw him from the bar upstairs and warned me he was on his way in. I hid in the kitchen." She picked up her coffee but didn't take a sip.

Instead, she gave Olive a hard look. "I'm done with Eddie Vance. It was less difficult to put down heroin than it was to get rid of him. I had no idea how much he was keeping me stuck in the insanity until we were done. I feel like I dumped the proverbial eight-hundred-pound gorilla on my back. It's fucking fabulous."

"It's too bad that rather than joining you in recovery, he's content to continue using and ultimately, to lose you," Olive said. "Do you think there's any chance this will be a wakeup call for Eddie? That he'll use it as a catalyst for change?"

"Eddie has been kicked off of every other methadone clinic in the city prior to West Street. He won't ever stop using. Eddie loves the lifestyle too much."

Olive knew she should refrain from discussing the details of another patient's treatment; it was always a tightrope walk when working with someone who had a family member or significant other on the clinic in terms of confidentiality issues, but Olive's next statement was a blatant violation of HIPPA.

"The Medical Director and nurses are aware that Eddie uses methadone not as it was intended, but as a substitute when he can't get his hands on heroin and wants to keep from getting sick. His drug screens make no secret of that."

If this admission by Olive surprised Nicole, she didn't show it. "I'm afraid things are going to get worse," Nicole said. "I heard through the clinic grapevine that Eddie's got a new connection. Some dealer that sold to three people in as many weeks, all who overdosed, one fatal. People are saying this guy's got *fire* on his hands, that the guys that handle it before him have been sprinkling a little fentanyl fairy dust into the supply." Nicole shuddered; Olive wasn't sure if it was in hypothetical anticipation or revulsion.

Olive typed out a quick note before turning back to Nicole. "Not to sound callous, but that's Eddie's problem. Or at the very least, Eddie's counselor's problem. My concern is you."

Nicole smiled and nodded, but she was twirling the obsidian ring on her finger in continuous, rapid circles.

"Seriously, Nicole," Olive caught her patient's eye, "you were unhappy with the situation you were in, so you took the necessary steps to change it. Nothing is more intimidating than change, and not only did you break one bad habit, you put down arguably the most addictive drug on the planet. Now that you're clean, my guess is that you'll be pretty much unstoppable. Speaking of which, did you start at Yard House yet?"

In addition to working at one of the most popular Italian restaurants in the North End, Nicole had recently been hired at one of the busiest bars near Fenway Park.

"I worked my first shift this past weekend. I made absolute bank. Over three-hundred dollars after tip-out in six hours. I'm working tonight, and the Sox are playing the Yanks at home. It's going to be a shit-show."

They chatted about the pros and cons of restaurant work, and Olive became cognizant that their exchange was more of a dialogue than a counselor-led affair, but Olive couldn't justify pummeling Nicole with questions about triggers and cravings and NA meetings when they'd already established how well she was doing. *Let sleeping dogs lie,* Olive thought. *Better yet, let dormant addicts be.*

At ten minutes to eleven, Olive plucked a card from the fresh stack and wrote out Nicole's appointment for the following week. She followed Nicole to the office door, but took a step back when Nicole flipped her head forward and reconstructed her intricate bird's nest of a hairdo.

"See you in group Friday," Nicole said. "You really are the best, you just get it, you know?" She juggled the mostly-empty coffee cup with her car keys and phone, not bothering to throw her belongings in the metal-studded purse.

"If you get a drug screen this week, it will be your last group," Olive said with a wistful smile. She watched Nicole walk down the hallway to the back exit—counselors were supposed to escort patients everywhere on the premises, but Olive loathed the authoritarian implications of the rule and avoided doing so when she could—and shut the door behind her.

Nicole was one of her favorite patients, but Olive was relieved to be alone. Anyone who wanted to see her would have to be buzzed back by the secretary, so there was no threat of disturbance from a perpetual no-call, no-shower deciding that now was the time they wanted to discuss their latest love triangle or legal issue.

She sank into her chair with a groan. The only downside to working at the clinic was the six AM start time; it never got any easier, even after three years on the same schedule. Olive didn't need a mirror to know she had bags under her eyes, and waitressing three nights a week didn't help matters.

Olive couldn't claim a North End or Fenway Park locale. She was stuck at The Living Room, a hipster hangout near Faneuil Hall that boasted couch-and-fireplace carrels instead of tables or booths. Last night had been Trivia Night; Olive hadn't escaped until after one AM, held hostage by a plaid-smothered couple whose never-ending IPAs were surpassed only by their never-ending espressos.

Olive took a sip of her own coffee, but it was cold. She didn't dare cross the lobby to nuke it, unwilling to trade the illusion that her session with Nicole had run late for a fresh cup. She slapped at the mouse to reanimate the dead computer and navigated to the Bank of America website. Her stomach knotted as she typed in her user name and password. She had to resist the urge to close her eyes as the page loaded.

She cringed when the account balance appeared on the screen. Olive tried to avoid logging in as much as possible for this exact reason. *How did it get so low?* She had some cash from the night before, but the ancillary income did little to alleviate the uphill climb that was living on a clinician's salary in Boston.

Olive patted her pocket. The wad of cash was too thin to offer up any real encouragement. Rent was due, and the electricity bill, and her student loan, and she hadn't bought groceries in what felt like months.

Her cell phone vibrated in her purse on the floor. Fishing it out, Olive saw *Mom and Dad - Home* flashing across the screen. She sent the call to voicemail. She stood and rolled back from the desk, dragged the tattered patient chair, still warm from where Nicole had sat, and retrieved a scarf from a hook on the back of her door. Propping her feet on the opposite chair, covering as much of her body with the scarf as she could, Olive leaned back and prepared to sleep through lunch.

She took a deep breath and pushed aside thoughts of negative account balances, phone calls from her parents, and Edward Vance. She had just drifted off when a commotion came from the hall.

"You can't go back there!" Cathy, the front-desk secretary, was yelling. Olive heard a grunt, followed by heavy breathing. Curious, she crept to the door. When no further sound came, she turned the knob.

The door was thrown open with such force, Olive stumbled backward, almost falling over the makeshift bed she'd fashioned in the center of the room. Eddie sneered at her from the threshold before stepping into her office. All the office doors in the clinical wing locked from the inside.

Eddie kicked back and the latched clicked.

It occurred to Olive that she should say something first, try to usurp the upper hand, despite the obvious fact of Eddie breaking into the back hall and barging into her office uninvited. She didn't get the chance.

"Who the fuck do you think you are?" Eddie's thick Boston accent unfurled from between still-sneering lips.

"Excuse me?" Olive hoped playing dumb would buy her some time. How had this lumbering idiot gotten past the security guard, the secretary, and the locked door from lobby to hallway in order to be standing in front of her with all the tranquility of a ticking time bomb?

Her attempt at ignorance did not work.

"Don't fuck with me. She was just here for her counseling appointment. I saw her at the gas station on Meridian Street."

Eddie swayed on his feet. It occurred to Olive that he'd been drinking on top of his usual mix of weed, heroin, and Xanax. Olive looked around Eddie's shoulder at the motionless door handle. *Why isn't anyone coming to help me?*

Eddie took a lurching step toward her.

"She told me about the new apartment. I made her tell me. I knew she wasn't at Linda's anymore. That dumb bitch mother of hers practically said as much. Where the hell am I supposed to live now, huh? She wouldn't even give me the address. Can you believe that? Of course you can, this whole fucking thing was your idea. Nik wouldn't have broken up with me if it wasn't for *you*."

He took another step forward and dug a meaty finger into her shoulder to punctuate his sentence. In the meager quarters of her office, this brought Eddie Vance a foot from where she stood, frozen in place. Olive could smell the musty aroma of stale cigarettes and wet dog. Nicole had always complained about Eddie's ever-expanding pack of pit bulls, dogs he collected like his many addictions, and pawned off on family members and running partners indiscriminately.

Olive heard activity mounting from the direction of the lobby. Her office was the first door on the right, the closest to the lobby door. *What is taking Cathy so long?* She was always losing her damn keys. For all she knew, Eddie had plucked the secretary's key ring right off her desk. *How else would this asshole have gotten back here?*

Briefly, Olive chastised herself for the harsh thought before realizing she had no desire to apply unconditional positive regard to this conversation, to this patient. She wasn't scared—not yet—but she also didn't care to see how far Eddie's anger would propel him.

"You think it's easy being me?" Eddie continued.

Now Olive decided that in addition to the weed, dope, Xanax, and booze, Eddie had stood in line for his dose before barging through the door to the back hallway. His eyelids drooped, and his tongue darted around his mouth, tasting the bitter remnants of medication.

"I had a girl who was taking care of me, who loved me. Without her, I'm just another junkie on the street. But you don't get that, do you? To you, my life is a game.

"You've never had to scramble for your next high, your next meal, a place to sleep at night. You learned everything you know from a big, fat counseling textbook and you preach your ideas, and hang up your fancy diplomas, and you give your advice, never thinking about how it affects actual people."

Olive heard a key turning in a lock now, not her door, but close. "I'm sorry you feel that way, Eddie," she said, and she meant it, but she was also biding her time until Pauley, the security guard, or Steve, the Clinical Director, or *someone* rushed in to rescue her.

"You bitch."

His tone had dropped several decibels. Olive felt the first twinge of fear. *Hurryuphurryuphurryup...*

"You're not sorry," Eddie said. "But I can make you sorry."

A click as a key penetrated the lock. Olive didn't exhale until Steve and Pauley burst into the room. Pauley had Eddie under the arms and halfway out the door before the intruding patient had time to turn and see who'd come for him. Pauley dragged Eddie down the hall toward the back exit to a chorus of profanities. Steve followed behind them, reading aloud from the emergency discharge paperwork clutched between his fingers.

I hope I wasn't waiting for reinforcements while Steve printed out the damn discharge spiel.

"You are not to come onto the property for any reason," Steve rattled off. If you come onto the property for any reason, West Street Neighborhood Health Center will notify the police and security will escort you from the premises. If deemed necessary, the clinic will press charges for trespassing. Due to the aggressive nature of your actions, you have forfeited the right to appeal your discharge."

Eddie had stopped fighting Pauley, who had a good hundred pounds on him, and was laughing quietly to himself, as if getting forcefully removed from the clinic was just about the funniest thing he had ever experienced. Steve ignored the laughter, eyes still on the printout.

"Your counselor will provide you with a list of treatment resources, mailed to the last home address you have listed on file. The Commonwealth of Massachusetts requires a signature on all forceful discharges, however if you refuse to sign the document, this does not negate the binding directives of said document.

"Mr. Vance, will you sign your discharge agreement?"

"Fuck you!" Eddie spat.

"Pauley, get him out of here," Steve said.

Olive guessed there were another few clauses to the emergency discharge, but Steve wouldn't be spending any more time on Eddie Vance. She retreated from her vantage point into her office, Steve close on her heels.

"Are you all right? What was that all about? What did he say to you?"

Olive heaved a shaky sigh. She stared at a hole in the plaster above Steve's head. The clinic hadn't bothered to repaint the office when she had been hired, and the hole was left over from the previous counselor who had occupied the office, the ghost of some proudly-hung diploma or framed Serenity Prayer.

When Olive first came to work at West Street, the hole in the plaster had exacerbated her obsessive-compulsive nature. She contemplated patching and painting over the scar herself, but now had bigger things to worry about than an imperfect paint job. Olive tried to focus her attention on Steve. She hoped to avoid a lengthy analysis of her confrontation with Eddie Vance, but knew this was unlikely.

Damn him, Olive thought. *There goes a quiet afternoon to myself.* What she said to Steve was, "I am Nicole Price's counselor for her one-to-one sessions. Eddie was her boyfriend. He thinks that it's my fault she broke up with him."

"Is this an ongoing issue with Nicole and Eddie? Why haven't you brought this up in supervision?"

Olive suppressed a groan. *For this precise reason*, she thought. *Because I do everything in my power to avoid your scrutiny.* "I didn't think he would escalate things. From what Nicole has said, he's all talk."

Steve's square jaw jutted into a disapproving frown. He pulled up the chair Olive had planned to nap in and took a seat. Olive attempted a clandestine glance at the clock on her desk. She fussed with her shirt sleeves, avoiding her boss's intrusive stare.

"We have discussed what can happen when you make assumptions that compromise safety, have we not?" Steve pushed back in his chair, his pant legs riding up to reveal the signature cowboy boots. As if an office full of Longhorns memorabilia wasn't enough, Steve liked to stress his affinity for all things Texas. Olive realized he had asked her something that required a response.

"Hmm? Oh. Yes, sorry, you're right. We have discussed it, yes."

"And?"

"Annnnd—" *And what?* Olive wasn't sure of the answer Steve was looking for. "And one should avoid making assumptions that compromise safety?" She parroted Steve's words back to him.

Steve's frown deepened. "I am talking about you, specifically, Olive. I am worried that you are inserting yourself into the lives of these patients so completely that you're becoming blind to where the line is. When that happens, counselor burnout is the least of your troubles. I'd be more worried about complete occupational fatigue, mental health issues; it's the kind of thing that sends people over the edge, pretending you're on the other side of the desk."

"What line?" Olive asked, before Steve could move ahead with the lecture.

"I'm sorry?"

"You said *you're becoming blind to where the line is.* What line?"

Steve leaned forward slightly. "The line between counselor and patient. The boundary that separates us from them. The—"

Olive cut him off. "Us from them? If that's a distinction I'm supposed to make, I'm not sure how comfortable I feel making it." She was pleased to see that Steve's face had gone a little pale.

"That's not... I just mean that you've got to maintain healthy boundaries per the moral and ethical codes of conduct we're governed by. I mean that if Nicole Price is dragging you too far into her personal melodrama, you have the right as her counselor to pump the breaks and redirect the session to a more productive line of communication. Does that make sense?"

Olive had harped on his mention of ethical codes, and scrambled to reorient herself with the direction the rest of his speech had gone in. When several seconds had passed, and Olive still had not responded, Steve peered at her closely and said, "Are you all right? Not just about what happened today, but in general, are you doing okay? I feel like you've been... quiet lately. You haven't been your usual peppy self. Is there anything you want to talk about? Anything at all?"

The skin on the back of Olive's neck prickled; Steve was her boss, not her shrink. He had a lot of nerve peppering her with such personal questions.

"I'm fine." Olive fidgeted with the sleeve of her shirt again. "I appreciate your concern though." She hoped she'd arranged her features in an expression that portrayed how fine she really was.

Steve checked his watch.

Yes, yes, say you have to go...

"I'm free until two," he said. "We can move to my office and discuss this further if you need to debrief. You'll have to write up an incident report of course. We can parse out the more salient points of what happened."

"Thank you, but I'm fine, really." The thought of being cloistered behind a closed door in that overwhelmingly orange office filled Olive with dread. She smiled, but her teeth were clamped together in a grimace. She willed him to leave. For one last agonizing moment, Steve sat, contemplating Olive with intensity, a zookeeper observing his chimp.

Finally, he stood. "What time is your next appointment?"

"One."

Steve nodded, as if he had expected this answer. "Use the next hour to get your head on straight. You know where to find me if you need me."

It took only a moment for Olive to decide she was done with counseling sessions for the remainder of the day. She pulled up her next appointment and dialed the telephone number listed in the patient's profile.

After listening to a recording prompting her to leave a message, Olive said, "Hey, Crystal, it's Olive. I'm really sorry, especially since I did this to you last week, but something has come up and I have to reschedule. I know that it's extremely short notice so please, give me a call back and whatever you have available, I promise I'll make work."

She hung up the phone, relief surging through her brain and limbs like a drug. *I need a little* me *time.* Olive reached for her keys and phone. *After the morning I've had, I can step out for a bit longer than usual. I deserve it.* With this justification in mind, she turned off her computer, flipped the light switch, and shut the door behind her.

Olive left the clinic every afternoon for a quick break, but this would be two weeks in a row that her break would extend into the one PM appointment block. Dosing hours were over and the clinic had the feel of a hospital after the first wave of a zombie apocalypse. It was so quiet, Olive wondered if Steve had evacuated the building during the incident with Eddie, and the patients who had been in with their counselors hadn't stuck around to resume sessions.

The clicks of Olive's three-inch heels echoed in the empty corridor as she headed for the same door Pauley had dragged Eddie out of twenty minutes prior. The air conditioning unit rattled like something had been trapped behind the grates and wanted out. Olive quickened her stride in anticipation of the early summer sun on her face. May had been cold, but June was fulfilling its promise of warm nights and beach-worthy days. She wished she'd taken today off; the vacation time she had scheduled next week couldn't come soon enough. A noise came from behind and Olive spun around, convinced for one terrible moment that Eddie had gotten back into the building and was poised to reach out and grab her. The door to the group room stood ajar, blown against the wall by a light breeze coming in through an open window. Shaking off her unease, Olive resumed her trek. She reached the end of the hall, pushed open the door, and stepped into the blinding light.

For several exhilarating seconds, Olive did get to enjoy the heat of the sun on her chilled skin, coupled with a dissociative pang of melancholy for not getting out and enjoying the world more. Then, the desire to get away from the clinic and the urgency of her errand overtook her, and she hopped into her Accord and drove out of the West Street parking lot.

Over the course of her mile-long journey, Olive kept the radio off. She did not hum or talk to herself, and she didn't bother turning to look out the window at the passing scenery. She *did* make a single phone call, and once satisfied that her errand would be rewarded, she silenced the cell phone and placed it in the middle console. She never noticed the car tailing her in the rearview mirror.

Olive pulled over on Warren Street and put the car into park, but did not shut off the engine. She reached for her cell, opened the door, and stepped outside, her shiny heels out of place on the trash-lined street. Circling the front of her car, Olive lifted her eyes to the third floor window of the building before her, squinting in the glare.

Something whizzed by her and clattered to the sidewalk on her right. When, on reflex, Olive turned to look, a swatch of black fabric was pulled over her head. Panicked, Olive reached out, but powerful arms encircled her, forcing her own arms to her sides and thwarting any further movement.

She tried to scream but the air caught in her throat. Before she could think, before she could reinflate her lungs, she was yanked backward with devastating speed, the arms around her torso joined by another set of hands at the ankles. Olive felt her feet lose contact with the earth at the same time she heard the Accord door open, and then she was thrown into the backseat of her own idling vehicle.

Olive sensed someone climbing in next to her before they rolled their impressive weight onto her lower body. She was lifted to a sitting position and something—*duct tape?*— was wound around her neck, effectively fastening her shroud. Her hands and feet were bound in a similar manner. The weight across her lap receded. The back door slammed shut. Both driver and passenger doors opened, then shut, and two male voices conversed in whispers too low for her to make out through her hood.

The driver pulled the Honda back out onto Warren Street, moving at what felt like an average but steady speed. Olive could hardly breathe, tensing every muscle in her body as if she'd been strapped into the car of a rollercoaster against her will and was about to drop over the first freefall.

Some section of Olive's brain as yet untouched by panic commanded her to pay attention to the direction the car turned in, if at all possible. They turned left at the end of the road, but thirty seconds later, Olive had lost all sense of direction in a city she knew well enough only to get to Warren Street, the clinic, the coffee shop, and the pharmacy. Olive bit her bottom lip to keep from crying out. She tried to calm down enough to think.

Someone will notice when I don't come back to the clinic. Steve will think the incident with Eddie upset me more than I let on and call to check in. But she knew this was not the case. There were plenty of afternoons that passed without anyone challenging her closed office door, patient or no patient. Steve may have expressed concern over the incident with Eddie, but Olive knew that at the end of the day, West Street's Clinical Director was more than ready to leave the facility, and all its drama, behind him.

Before she could catastrophize any further, the Accord slowed, then came to a stop. Olive allowed herself a small measure of relief at the relatively short distance her captors had travelled. If she had to bet, she'd wager they were still in

Chelsea; maybe an escape route would present itself, and she could find a recognizable landmark to guide her out of this nightmare.

"Get her out," the voice from the passenger seat said. There was no denying who that voice belonged to.

It was Eddie Vance.

"The fuck, man? What the fuck do you think this is? I snatched her. I drove. This was your idea. You want her out, you get her the fuck out."

Olive thought she recognized the voice of Eddie's accomplice, but she couldn't place it without seeing his face. The driver and passenger doors opened, then shut. The door at her head opened. Rough hands jostled for position beneath her armpits, clamping together a half inch below the underwire of her bra. The hands became fists and dug painfully into her ribcage as she was dragged headfirst from the backseat.

Deposited onto the pavement, Olive wobbled on her heels. The hands moved from under her breasts to her shoulders to steady her, but the gesture was devoid of benevolence.

"Walk, bitch," Eddie commanded. Something cold and hard was pressed into the small of her back. "Don't make me unsheathe my pocket knife."

In spite of her fear, Olive almost laughed. No doubt Eddie was enjoying this real-life version of *Grand Theft Auto*.

She staggered forward, each blind footfall more anxiety-provoking than the last. As she walked, she felt the unexpected sensation of the tape giving way at the back of her neck. The restrictive hood became a piece of flapping fabric, loosely-fastened. Eddie couldn't have noticed, for he continued guiding her forward. Olive tried to move in a way that would facilitate loosening the fabric further without attracting his attention, an effort made easier by her lurching, tentative gait.

The pavement ceased. Olive faltered, her heels spiking through the gravel to the layer of soft dirt below. She pressed on, fighting for balance. Her shroud was not completely opaque; she sensed the moment when she was led beneath the shadow of a looming edifice, the sun extinguished like a candle snuffed out by a too-eager breath on a birthday. Fear moved in to fill the spaces in her brain made vacant by departing rationality. Fear that, though primal, had been tinged with confusion and hope; now that fear was short-circuited by a bolt of panic; if she disappeared into whatever structure waited ahead, she was as good as lost.

Olive jerked to a halt and tossed her head forward, slipping the hood. Her lack of hesitation, the refusal to consider what would happen if her plan backfired, giving her the advantage of speed and therefore, surprise. Eddie reached down in a clumsy attempt to reclaim his grip on her shoulder, but grabbed a fistful of pearls instead. Olive faked a turn to the left, ducking out of Eddie's reach. She felt a mild sensation of resistance, and then the necklace gave and she was free, an explosion of pearls raining onto the gravel below. She darted right. She did not waste her energy on a scream.

In an adrenaline-fed state of hypervigilance, Olive took in her surroundings: it could have been any street, in any town, east of the city. Two-family houses lined both sides with cold indifference, their empty windows witnessing her flight without producing a blink of shutter or streaming sash.

Olive reached the road. The swell of adrenaline had converged; her pupils widened to take in all available light, twin pools that have overflown after a deluge of rain. She risked a ninety-degree glance to her left, but the empty street offered nothing by way of escape. Nowhere to hide. Unwilling to waste another second, she sprinted to the right. She thought she detected the whir of an engine coming from that direction. The muscles in her thighs bunched like loaded springs. The acidic, yellowy taste of bile crept up the back of her throat.

I can do this. There was no sign of Eddie in her periphery, no pounding of footsteps over the rush of blood in her ears. The road curved and Olive could see a through street running perpendicular to the road on which she ran. She could almost make out the street sign up ahead. Another few strides and it would become visible through the low-hanging branches of a massive oak. Cars whizzed by at frequent intervals. Olive's heart leapt. She did not see the flash of white through blue blossoms of a rhododendron on her right.

Eddie's tackle blindsided her. The last thing she saw before his weight took her to the pavement in a crushing wave of knocking bones and tearing flesh was a van crossing the intersection. It sped through like an image on a movie screen, the sun catching the lacquered metal and turning it into liquid gold.

—

The sound drifted up through the black water of her subconscious like the cranking of a great barge. Coupled with her nausea, it occurred to Olive that perhaps she was being lowered into the belly of that barge, and her limbs searched for purchase like those of a panicked dog heading toward the dreaded bathwater. Her fingernails caught the wall, where the craterous concrete tore the nails from her middle and ring fingers in one smooth rip. Olive shrieked, but found her throat produced no sound. Something filled her mouth, pressing her tongue into the backs of her bottom teeth so that all she could manage was an animalistic growl. Her eyelids flickered. The black water became an ocean of grey at the same moment the pressure around her ribcage increased. Olive squirmed. The pressure shifted.

"Fuck," a voice said. "She's awake. Hurry and get her down."

The pressure resumed its previous intensity. The pace at which she was being lowered quickened. Olive felt her feet slap off one gritty, wooden stair after another. A protruding nail pierced the soft flesh below her ankle bone, drawing blood. The angle of her descent was altered. Her boat coasted over calmer seas. The two men scrambled to cross the room's not insignificant length with their human baggage before dumping her into a pile of foul-smelling bedding on the floor.

Like a fish left on a dock, Olive flailed, gagging at the musty fabric pressed against her mouth. She sucked in a lungful of fresh air through her nose to find it was only slightly better than the mildew clinging to the comforters. The smell reminded Olive of the pumpkin that had rolled off her porch last Halloween, left to fester in a pile of damp leaves after a rainstorm. When she'd unearthed it by its near-putrefied stem, the smell that had accosted her was akin to what she smelled now. The sickly-sweet smell of rot, unsusceptible to even the most astringent of cleaning products. It was the smell of rats that had died between walls, sealed up to decay at their leisure.

She shook her head, trying to evade the stench and clear the panic that infiltrated her grey matter like cobwebs. Eddie was dragging something across the cement floor to the center of the room. Footsteps disappeared up the stairs behind her. Or was it to the left? The echoes that bounced off the basement walls like children playing hide-and-seek played tricks on Olive's ears. She *was* in a basement, that much she could discern.

And she had to find a way out.

Olive's hands tingled behind her back. She rolled forward to take the weight off her wrists and flexed the fingers. The injured nailbeds protested vehemently. She tested her binds; the rope which held her felt no thicker than the drawstring of a hooded sweatshirt. She strained against the knot, working it loose.

"I don't fucking think so," Eddie said.

Olive flinched and opened her eyes.

"Pull all you want, but this time, you're not going anywhere."

Eddie reached for her. Olive shrank back, but he'd already taken the edge of the sodden comforter in his hands and begun dragging her along the concrete toward the center of the room. There sat a solitary chair of the patio furniture variety, poised like an unwanted throne. Olive tried to scramble backward, but Eddie caught her ankle and reeled her in. He scooped her up without effort and deposited her into the chair. A roll of duct tape materialized like a prop in a macabre magic trick.

Eddie the Magnificent. Olive's brain recoiling from the reality of what was happening. *Watch as he makes the counselor next door disappear, right before your eyes!*

She made a last ditch effort to launch herself from the chair, but Eddie pushed her down, turned, and sat, pinning her beneath him. He peeled the edge of the tape free with his teeth and wound the roll around each of her wrists. Still on top of her, he bent forward to secure her ankles.

He sat up and leaned back, pressing the side of his face to hers. When he spoke, his lips moved against her cheek like slugs. His breath was hot, smelled sour.

"Not a bad seat I've got here. You know, for a snotty bitch who doesn't know half as much as she thinks she does, you're still one hot piece of ass. Too bad part of my plan is to get back with Nicole, otherwise I'd take you for a spin myself. See if that fancy diploma of yours is good for more than book smarts."

Olive's expression remained wooden. She was desperate to mask her fear, but knew Eddie could feel her shaking beneath him. Mercifully, he stood, smirked, and retraced all four tape jobs with a meticulousness she couldn't imagine he employed within any other facet of his life.

With each decisive tear of tape, the bleakness of her predicament grew. Anything short of a recently-sharpened box cutter would be insufficient in facilitating her escape.

Even if she'd had a tool, she knew Eddie would never give her an opportunity to use it.

He rolled the tape toward a set of shelves, where it disappeared into a murky crevasse curtained by cobwebs. He scanned the basement, betraying no more concern for the woman bound to a chair at the center of the room than any other item in the dimly-lit cellar. It was coming, now, whatever it was he had planned for her. She braced herself for pain, for degradation and terror, humiliation and despair.

To her tremendous surprise and relief, Eddie turned, and disappeared up the basement steps without another word.

Bound, gagged, terrified, and alone, the distinction between seconds, minutes, and hours ceased to exist. The squat basement windows were too coated with grime to note any change in the sun's position, or if the sun still shone at all. Olive's dungeon—Olive's morale—existed in a vacuum of the blackest night, void of sun, moon, or stars.

So Olive sat. Besides worry, she could do nothing. Her bones ached. Her stomach churned. Her eyes smarted with each new bout of tears. She tried to empty her mind. She tried not to panic. She tried to avoid imagining what Eddie had in store for her. She couldn't fathom the possibility that he would kill her. But what would stop her from going to the police if he let her go? Still, how many times had Nicole Price filled an entire session by discussing Eddie Vance's lack of initiative?

If he wasn't going to kill her, what then? Olive's brain churned out one appalling prospect after another until her body was unable to sustain the elevated epinephrine and cortisol levels, and she crashed into depression. She might have slept, but the numbness she was suspended in was probably closer to a state of shock. When footsteps fell on the bulkhead stairs—the ones she had been dragged down either two minutes or two hours earlier—Olive did not register them until the descending sneaker-thuds hit the bottom two steps.

The gag had dried in her mouth and her throat felt like a tunnel of cast Paper Mache. Eddie moved into her line of vision. Again, Olive thought of a magician stepping onstage to greet his audience. He placed something behind a plastic bin of Christmas decorations before coming at her with the loose-limbed gait of a man in the throes of a hefty dose of narcotics. He loosened a strip of duct tape from the roll, and pulled it taut. He inspected her as if she were an ant; Eddie was the bully with the magnifying glass.

Olive's wrists, ankles, and mouth were already restrained. Before she could guess at which body part Eddie planned to tape up next, he had slapped the adhesive across her chest and wound it around her back, pinning her upper arms to her sides tight enough so that breathing was a concentrated effort. Olive tried to flex her muscles while Eddie circumnavigated her torso, remembering something she had read once and hoping that if she loosened her muscles by degrees, air would flow into her lungs more freely.

"Well, well, well," Eddie said. His stubbled face was flushed. "I told you that you'd be sorry, didn't I? Look at you. Not so high and mighty without your boss or your body guard to bail you out."

He moved at her with a speed she would never have

imagined he'd possessed, synthetic-opioid-slowed speech and a flabby physique masking some innate, inexplicable agility.

"I made up my mind to teach you a lesson after Nicole broke up with me. The bullshit at the clinic today was the final straw."

He jammed his hands into his pockets and glared at her. "I know your type. Just because you wouldn't give me the time of day doesn't mean I don't know what you're all about. I wouldn't want a girl like you anyway. High-fucking-maintenance, oodles of that student loan debt, never satisfied, always whining about things not being good enough when you have everything.

"I'd take a girl like Nicole over you any day. Nik's down for whatever. She's easygoing, but works hard for what she has. At least, she used to be. Until you ruined her with your ideas."

Eddie reached behind the bin of holiday cheer to retrieve what he had hidden there. Though his sausage fingers dwarfed the object, and the light in the basement was dim, Olive could see what he held. The color gave it away. The same color as a Dunkin Donuts straw. Her session with Nicole that morning seemed like it had been months ago. With effort, Olive tore her gaze from the hypodermic needle to look Eddie in the eye. She mumbled something through the gag.

Eddie stepped forward and ripped the tape from her mouth. Olive goaded her sluggish tongue to life, eradicating the bunched-up cloth from between her lips like a Novocained patient post-root canal.

"Wha—wha... why?"

"I told you why."

It did not take long for Olive to discover the reason Eddie had applied the last layer of duct tape. No matter how hard she tried, no matter which way she manipulated her body, she was unable to thwart his impending efforts. Worse, the tape itself was acting as a tourniquet; the veins in her arms were already pronounced. *Like shooting fish in a barrel.*

Still, she struggled, until Eddie, needle poised an inch over her arm, pointed out in a matter-of-fact tone, "You *will* take your medicine. The only thing thrashing around like that is going to do is cause me to miss my mark. Do that enough times, and... you ever seen *Requiem for a Dream*?"

She stopped struggling.

Eddie inserted the needle into her vein.

Olive watched as her blood exploded in the chamber like a tiny fireworks display.

He pressed the plunger down.

The fireworks display was in her head.

Waxy lids closed over dilated eyes. Goosebumps broke out along her exposed flesh. A small pinprick of blood lay in the crook of her elbow like a pearl in the milky dish of an oyster shell.

Eddie took an uncertain step back. The look on his face suggested he'd considered this plan only up until the moment of injection and now had no idea how to react to the woman ascending to the highest peak of euphoria before him.

Olive's eyelids flickered. Concern flashed across Eddie's porcine features. He stepped toward Olive, one hand outstretched as if to take her pulse, then stopped. Olive shuddered, turned to one side, and vomited a stream of brown liquid onto the concrete floor. Her chin rested on her chest, which rose and fell slowly.

The last thing Olive heard was the sound of Eddie's footsteps clamoring up the stairs like a child running from a well-deserved punishment. The noise registered as something she should pay attention to, but couldn't summon the energy to concern herself with, like the sound of her mother calling for her when she'd played in the back garden of her childhood home and didn't want to come in for supper. Before she could decide if the footsteps were indeed important, they were gone.

After another measured, strenuous breath, it was as if they had never been there at all.

—

Light.

Light flooded the previously dark world. Olive had fallen while mountain climbing and a rescue team shone their lights into the craggy canyon in which she was trapped.

No, that wasn't quite right. Olive strained against the fog, trying to remember where she was. The truth had made it to the edge of her awareness when the light went out again.

No, that wasn't right either. The light persisted, but Olive had closed her eyes. She took a breath and forced them open, shocked at how much effort it took to command muscles previously governed by reflex.

The integrity of the light source established, its illumination was both lovely and loathsome, bringing with it the end of uncertainty—*Mother is home, run to the door to greet her!*—and the onset of a dismal alarm—*the bus is here, the bus is here, get up, Olive, it's time for school.* Her tongue felt fuzzy, as if an insane artist had sketched her in pencil before deciding to erase her mouth. Her arms and legs were enduring waves of pins and sewing machine-powered needles, jackhammering through her skin into once-tough flesh, now tenderized.

Olive could've been convinced that what was formerly her brain had become an organ of reverence, removed from her skull by idolaters to be preserved in an embalming fluid of analgesic vapor. If euphoric mummification was not its fate, than perhaps her brain had been turned into a vat of strawberry jelly, crafted from the ripest, juiciest berries and baked between layers of puff pastry, warm and buttery and pliable and delicious.

A shadow fell across the light on the basement floor and Olive murmured something inaudible. Though she'd perceived his footsteps on the last two stairs, it seemed to Olive that Eddie materialized from thin air. Blinking in confusion, Olive alternately doused and reignited the sun in the shoebox diorama that was her universe.

"Well, you're not dead," Eddie said. His voice conveyed neither relief nor surprise. "You're not dead," he said again. "So how did you like your medicine?"

Olive saw Eddie's mouth move, but someone had disconnected the auxiliary cord that ran from her eyes to her ears. Or maybe it was the cord that connected her ears to her brain?

Her lack of reply did little to discourage him. "It is not exactly an acquired taste. If I had to guess, I'd say you enjoyed it quite a bit. And that was only your very first dose." Eddie laughed a snorting, piggish laugh.

The laugh succeeded in reconnecting her sensory sound system.

"You'll graduate from enjoyment to full-on love affair soon enough," Eddie said. He eyed the vomit on the floor with distaste. "Everyone throws up their first time. Then again, that was some good shit I gave you. A regular user may very well have booted it after shooting what I gave you. That stuff is *fire*."

Olive watched Eddie pick at something wedged between the crooked tombstones of his teeth. He stared at her over the substantial surface of his hand, then, as if he had only just remembered, said "Speaking of fire, I brought you round two."

That auxiliary cord must have a kink in it again because Eddie's words skipped in her head like a scratched record on a gramophone. Olive regarded the syringe pinched between nicotine-stained fingers. The thoughts that swirled through her head were indecipherable.

Eddie stepped forward, his satisfaction evident. "It's like a science experiment," he said. "Watching someone like *you* turn into someone like *me*."

Her lips strained to form some plea or protest, but their meaning was lost when Eddie leaned over her, squinting as he inserted the needle into the same vein as before, reopening the puncture wound to inject the pale brown liquid.

Olive's brain knew what to expect, anticipated the sensual rush of sweeping warmth that washed over her

114

body.

A small smile touched the corners of her lips. Other than that smile, she did not move.

—

Movement.

Above, coming from upstairs.

Olive swam toward it, the water parting around her, flowing over her skin without temperature, taste, or odor. Breaking the surface, Olive blinked water from her eyes to find that it had evaporated upon hitting the air, vanished like the commotion from above. From behind the basement windows, a pale glow hinted at either morning or a blinding full moon, with no way of telling which.

She shuddered, and the duct tape cut into her wrists. The sensation was uncomfortable, but not painful; the last dose of heroin had yet to wear off. Olive concentrated on pinpointing the noises. After several long moments, the back and forth of pacing footsteps announced themselves, accompanied by muffled voices, their inflection and tone implying anger, or at least impatience. She could discern nothing else through the ceiling beams, and lowered her gaze to evaluate her environment.

My prison, not my environment. I'm being held prisoner here.

Her conscious mind accepted this amendment, but the sentiment accompanying it was fleeting. The sharp edge of fear that had penetrated her every thought, pre-injection, had been blunted.

Olive knew she should explore this further, should analyze the reasons *why* fear was no longer her predominant emotion, but the issue didn't seem as pressing as she supposed it should. She turned her head as far as the restraints would allow, only to be reacquainted with the dirty laundry that had been her landing strip upon her initial descent down the bulkhead stairs. It looked softer and more inviting than she remembered.

Past the discarded linens, a set of metal shelves stretched from floor to ceiling. These contained the typical assortment of basement-delegated goods; cleaning supplies were interspersed with a myriad of holiday decorations, gardening tools hung from hooks on the wall, and a pink tricycle, matching hula-hoops, and a tangled spider web of jump ropes suggested little girls past the age of toddlerhood. In addition to these shelves so representative of normalcy, a home gym gleamed from the far corner, arranged on the quintessential puzzle-piece black foam mats.

Where am I? According to Nicole, Eddie couldn't afford a shitty studio; this looked to be the basement of a good-sized home, owned by people who could afford fancy gym equipment and expensive shelving units to house their off-season knick-knacks. Rows of clear storage bins showcased piles of well-organized children's books, toys, cookbooks, fishing equipment, backyard BBQ accouterments, and countless other indicators of a normal American family living normal American lives.

Only two possibilities, Olive surmised. Either the couple— a couple with at least one child—whose home she was being held in was implicated in her kidnapping and subsequent drugging. Or Eddie had broken into an empty house in order to carry out his plot.

Olive grasped at murky memories of counseling sessions

prior to Nicole and Eddie's breakup. She thought she could trust a vague recollection of the previous November, and the crazy gesticulations Nicole had engaged in while telling Olive of their nightmare Thanksgiving at Eddie's brother and sister-in-law's.

The pair had gotten so high before dinner that Eddie had nodded out with a serving spoon of mashed potatoes still in hand. Eddie's two nieces had found his apparent narcolepsy hilarious, but Nicole had been mortified, Olive remembered. Nieces would explain the pink tricycle and boxes of toys, but if this was Eddie's brother's place, where was Eddie's brother?

The possibility that they were on a weeklong vacation— similar to her post-Memorial Day time off planned for the upcoming week—felt like being tackled to the pavement all over again. The awful probability of this scenario cut through any lingering euphoria, and Olive felt the tips of her fingers turn to icicles on the arms of her chair.

A house conveniently unoccupied for the next week, and her with a time-off request already on the books, the final piece of the puzzle that would come together with no one knowing that Olive was even missing fell into place: Olive's behavior, her recent withdrawal from her parents, would hardly facilitate panic on their part. Not answering the phone when her parents called was one symptom of a larger, more complex condition. Olive hadn't been home in months.

Olive spun an amber ring around one finger, remembering when she'd sat across from Nicole in her warm, safe office, watching her patient engaged in the same nervous tic. Had Eddie given Nicole the obsidian ring, maybe years ago, before spending money on jewelry was still a plausible gesture?

Olive's boyfriend of four months—their meeting the only benefit Olive could attribute to working at The Living Room—had given Olive the amber ring on her birthday. The ring was a perfect symbol for their relationship: agreeable, understated, and less-than-resolute. If he didn't hear from her over the course of her vacation, Richard might wonder where she'd disappeared to, but he wouldn't worry, and he certainly wouldn't call the police. Olive's commitment to Richard was capricious at best.

And the clinic. Would anyone at the clinic realize that Olive had gone missing the same day as Eddie's involuntary discharge? Again, Olive didn't believe they would. As far as the staff at the clinic was concerned, Olive had left early for a week's vacation after a rough day at work.

The ceiling creaked above her again and Olive winced. She was uncomfortable, but apathetic, hungry, but none too worried about eating. *Will Eddie inadvertently starve me to death in his quest to turn me into an addict?* Then, a primal, unspeakable thought: *Is he going to rape me?*

The idea produced a feeling of foreboding in the marrow of her bones stronger than she would have thought possible. Olive longed for her previous state of incoherence before chastising herself for this repulsive, counterproductive thought. The cloud cover hanging over her consciousness had dissipated and terror took shape. Navigating her thoughts was like traversing a topiary maze, where stagnant bushes morphed into leering, stalking beasts.

Olive's breathing quickened. Light-headedness returned

full-force. The sound of footsteps hit the top stair, and began to descend, one nail in her coffin after another. Eddie appeared before her. *Poof,* Olive thought. *Eddie the Magnificent, coming to you live.* He stopped in front of her chair, tapping the toe of one Timberland, lips stretched into a lecherous smile.

Eddie's hand darted out toward hers. The sound reached her ears before the pain had registered—*POP!*—and the tape that had been sliced in two was left dangling from one numb and bloodless wrist. Olive was staring at the burst blood vessels rising in the aftermath of having the pocket knife forcefully inserted between tape and flesh when—*POP!*—Eddie knifed through the remaining shackle.

She raised her eyes to find him picking sticky remnants from the blade. He was panting slightly, as if he'd over-exerted himself coming down the basement stairs, and looked like he was waiting for her to acknowledge her newfound freedom by fighting. His expression twisted into one of wicked glee when instead of lashing out, he noticed Olive's eyes searching his empty hands.

"It's happening," he said, rubbing those hands together like a mad scientist. "You're fiending for it. Probably your body will take to it even quicker, being in the situation you're in. Defense mechanism, or some Sigmund Freud shit like that. Not that I'm complaining, mind you. The less time it takes to turn you into a full-fledged junkie, the less dope I have to share."

Sandpaper lined Olive's throat, but she managed to croak out a single word: "How?"

"How?" Eddie repeated. He looked perplexed. "How

what? How did I grab you from Warren Street? I was going to tail you when you went home for the day, but you left the clinic early, so I followed you then."

One hand disappeared behind his back, then reappeared to produce a tin foil parcel (*Eddie the Magnificent!*), nearly flattened by its journey from ground floor to basement in the confines of Eddie's pocket. He unwrapped the dented foil to reveal two slices of sloppily-buttered toast, which Eddie inspected the way a chef examines a gourmet entrée prior to its departure from the five-star kitchen in which it was forged.

He held the bread to her lips. Its sodden appearance, coupled with the smell of singed yeast and flour made her want to gag.

"Eat," he said.

Cardboard would have had more appeal, but she opened her mouth and allowed Eddie to shove the food between her lips. At first contact with the crumbly, alien texture, Olive's tongue recoiled; a moment later, her cheeks moved up and down in conjunction with her slow, methodic chewing.

"My boy helped nab you in exchange for some of the same shit you've been catching a habit with. If you mean how am I getting you high on top of my own habit, that answer is simple."

Eddie gestured to the walls around them, to the house they currently occupied. "My brother is as yet unaware that Nik let some know-it-all counselor talk her into breaking up with me. A few days ago, he texted her and asked if she would house-sit for the week following Memorial Day. My brother was *also* unaware that I swiped Nik's cell phone before she bounced. I had to sell mine, and Nik makes so much waitressing, she can afford a new phone no problem. I figured she wouldn't miss it.

"So Scott asks her if the two of us would stay here while he goes up to Maine or Vermont, or some bullshit state up in the mountains, with his picture-perfect family. He asks her to keep an eye on me, to make sure I don't pawn any of his priceless shit. Scott received a message back confirming that *yes, we'd be happy to watch his house for the week*, and *no, he didn't have to worry about a single, solitary thing*. I told him— or rather, *Nicole* told him—that we're both on the clinic now and doing really, really well." Eddie's tone conveyed how pleased he was with pulling off this deception.

He pushed the toast toward Olive's slack jaw and she ventured another bite. It was cold, on top of being burnt, but she was surprised by the growls her stomach produced now that she'd activated her anaesthetized metabolism.

She took a deep breath, swallowed hard, and said, "Ahhmph—"

Olive concentrated on the necessary facial muscles, and tried again. "Aaa—and when he comes back?"

Eddie shrugged, his expression shrewd. "Scott will get a text informing him that we had to leave for work. Then I'll stage a break-in. He'll probably still suspect it was me, but there'll be no proof. Besides, I know the guy who owns the pawn shop on Broadway. We've been tight ever since I helped him beat the shit outta some Southie scum a few years back. Punks broke into the store and shattered a bunch of display cases."

Eddie grinned, and Olive wondered at what point in his

drug use his teeth had taken on their current level of rot.

"He's on the clinic too," Eddie continued. "Gary Hansen. You know him?"

Olive said nothing. She'd had Gary in group once or twice; he was mandated for dirty drug screens, but rarely showed. Olive didn't see how this was Eddie's business. The week of his brother's vacation would end soon enough, and what did he plan to do with her then? If he wasn't going to let on, she wasn't interested in small talk. Before she could maneuver her slothful tongue into forming the words, Eddie tossed the toast over his shoulder and stood.

"You know, I was thinking earlier about your pearl necklace. The one I accidentally broke when you tried to run away. I'm sorry about that, but to be honest, now that I've gotten to know you, you don't really strike me as a pearls kinda girl."

Eddie's hand disappeared behind his back again.

Watch the amazing, stupendous, fantastical Eddie the Magnificent as he facilitates a trick beyond your wildest comprehension!

A syringe of Dunkin Donuts orange appeared.

Olive closed her eyes.

"Look at you," he laughed. "You're mine, I could put you on the lawn and you wouldn't go anywhere." She felt a tiny pinch.

The world's most efficient cleaning service came rushing in, countless maids sweeping feather dusters across her mind, obscuring the monstrous, looming shapes, and draping sheets over the sharp-edged furniture.

—

Olive dreamed that she was free. She was returning home to her apartment, anxious to put the harrowing ordeal of the last week behind her. Eddie Vance's face kept appearing on billboards along the side of the highway, and her heart only stopped its imitation of a moth beating itself against the glass walls of its lantern prison when she pulled off the exit for Overlook Ridge.

The left-hand turn to her complex a mere three-hundred feet away, she almost relaxed, approaching a police car with a black pickup truck pulled over in front of it. The driver of the pickup was standing next to a police officer who leaned against the hood of the cruiser and...

Olive jerked forward in her seat and stared. Even with everything she had been through, even amongst the mayhem and the horror and the breakdown of her world, the sight of the pickup driver aiding a police officer in tying off and injecting a syringe in the crook of his arm left her flabbergasted. She did not comprehend the sound of her own muttering, but as she pulled onto Terrace Road, past the red-rocked cliffs of the quarry that skirted her complex, she repeated to herself, "There's no place like home, there's no place like home."

The first building in her complex was as it had always been, the tan and burnt-orange brick fortress blocking the identical second set of apartments behind it. But the second building should have blocked her building from view, as the first building had blocked the second. Instead, a monstrously peaked black roof pitchforked up into a sky that was dark, and growing darker.

Gone was the impeccably landscaped front yard and

walkway, replaced by looming rock structures, grey, dismal, and connected to one another by thick iron chains. Black mud and fissures of wet earth gurgled in the mist, and the great-winged shadow of a vulture moved across the ground in the last of the dying sunlight. The building itself was a castle straight from Hell; any nightmare that manufactured that structure would have been banished to the dreamer's subconscious, never to see the light of day.

Its roofline was a tortured soul, carved and gutted and pierced into things it should never have been. Two lights blazed in twin windows above a horrible pit of a door, their luminescence glowing purple against an otherwise colorless world.

Olive's Accord moved through the gate and approached that hellish front door through no doing of her own. As the car slowed to a stop in front, the air inside became unbreathable, suddenly thick and too cloying to move in and out of her lungs. She threw herself from the car, trembling as her feet sunk into the black mud.

The infernal door opened with a hideous groan, like the sound of a hundred bones breaking under diseased skin. Olive could not avert her eyes. She heard the footsteps before she saw him, thousands of syringes dangling from both arms, Nicole, half-naked and chained at his side.

"I told you," he said, each word taking the same amount of time to utter as the one that preceded it. "I told you you'd be sorry. Now come here and take your medicine..."

—

If Olive's life had depended on it, and in a way it did, she could never have determined how many times, over how many days, Eddie flooded her veins with the beautifully noxious heroin. Her existence seemed to take on a dreamlike quality, and even the temperate ebbs and flows of her highs—*temperate* being the one factor that seemed to allude to Eddie never letting more than a few hours go by without visiting her in her dungeon dwelling—seemed blunted from being experienced in their absolute values. Rather, everything seemed hypnagogic, blurred, ambiguous.

That she was no longer taped to the chair hardly mattered, but the locked basement door and immovable windows were as severe a barrier to escape as any in her apathetic state. Eddie had bombarded Olive with such a constant stream of heroin, that her now natural state was now one of platitude. A prisoner held hostage via liquid handcuffs. Eddie could have left the door wide open and Olive would have lay placidly among the dirty comforters on the concrete floor, awaiting her next dose.

And on what was the seventh day of Olive's captivity, he did just that. The door stood open on its hinges, the light from the upstairs forming a triangular spotlight on Olive, lying in the fetal position on a urine-stained rug. When she didn't run off on her own accord, Eddie took to shouting at her like one would a tiresome dog, and finally, when there was still no movement from the thin form, he pulled her up, her stance that of a drunken sailor, and slogged her up the stairs, her bare, dirty feet bouncing off each step like a child dragging a Barbie doll behind her by the hair.

Upstairs, Eddie discovered that Olive was still too high to walk. He left her sleeping on the couch for a few hours while he played video games next to her, a frat boy waiting for his overly intoxicated coed to wake up and fulfill her end of their one-night stand bargain.

When she stirred, he scooped her up, deposited her onto the backseat of her car, and drove halfway to the clinic from his brother's empty house.

—

Olive sat up, a reanimated corpse. Bride of Morphine. Her Accord idled on a deserted side street. Behind the wheel, Eddie had a cigarette in one hand, a beer in the other. A roach simmered in the ashtray. Comprehension fought through the fog for the first time in days. Understanding affected her gaunt features.

"Welcome back to the real world." The wicked glee that had seemed to drive Eddie one week prior had been replaced by a grim resignation. "Go. Feel free to go straight to the cops, though I suspect you are of sound enough mind, even now, to realize that if you went to the police with your story, they would lock you up in the psych ward and throw away the key. You would look like the run-of-the-mill junkie, frantic and out of dope, but an imaginative one, desperate for sympathy, and maybe the fast track to a hard-to-come-by detox bed."

Eddie puffed on his cigarette. "I have a hunch that there's only one thing you're interested in pursuing anyway." He leaned over and retrieved something from the glove compartment.

"Here's a little going away present from me to you. There's enough cash here for one of two things. Gas, or cab money, to St. Elizabeth's detox. Or... a bag of heroin. And in case you choose door number two, I have something else for

126

you." He reached over the center console into the backseat and dropped the cash and a piece of folded-up paper into her lap. "Dealer's number, on me. They usually don't accept new customers without a difficult and time-consuming interview process of sorts. But I was such a good customer this week that you are in luck."

Eddie checked the rearview mirror before opening the door. Olive's window was open, and when he leaned in and gestured for her to pick up the cash and number, the smoke from his cigarette met with the remnants of the previous exhale, giving Olive the impression that she was caught in some sort of smoke-tornado. She groped with listless fingers for the money, and tucked the notepaper in with the bills without discrimination.

Eddie opened her door and pulled her out by the shoulders. "Oopsie daisy," he said. "Oh, I almost forgot. Here are your keys and your cell phone. I even charged it for you. Now you have everything you need to solve your little dilemma. If it can even be considered as such."

He smiled a final, nasty smile at her as he pushed her toward the driver's door. "My guess is that, if you even make it back to your cushy little counseling job at the clinic, you'll be singing a slightly different tune. Having to make it through life with this monkey on your back, having to survive as a dope fiend, let's see if you are so quick to judge, Miss Ahhllliiiveee."

He pronounced her name like the over-the-counter pain reliever. Olive felt like she was listening to him from under water. Before she realized that his monologue was over, he had walked halfway up the block. Olive watched him disappear around Webster Avenue, one street up.

Her head spun. *I could use some Aleve*, she thought wildly, her brain grasping at nonsensical connections, nerve endings misfiring in confusing spurts and starts. *No, I could use some...*

She put her hands in her pockets and pulled out the wad of cash in one, and her cell phone in the other. *I could go home*, she thought. *Go home and call a friend, or call Richard. Tell him what happened. Tell someone what happened. Or I could go to the hospital, be treated like any other individual who was the victim of violence. After all, I was kidnapped, attacked, assaulted.*

She stopped moving, realizing she had spun in innumerable circles, pondering what to do. She squared her shoulders. Her jaw knotted into a tense ball of bouncing muscle.

Olive picked up her cell phone. She needed to call someone who would help her. She needed to call someone who would take care of her and her burdensome affliction.

She dialed.

A voice answered on the third ring. In as condensed a version as possible, she explained what had happened. The voice murmured in understanding. Said he would be right there. Olive hung up.

A gold minivan, pulled up to the opposite side of the street from where Olive sat, perched expectantly on the curb. As she approached the window, she saw the driver's face register shock and dismay at her appearance. Olive bent toward the side mirror and surveyed her skeletal and bedraggled visage.

No matter, Olive thought. She was a short time away from being able to experience a heightened reality... where appearances did not matter.

"How much you want?" he asked her.

Olive reached her hand through the open window, and told the dealer to name his price.

——

Olive unlocked the door and let herself into the quiet room. She fidgeted with her shirt sleeve as she looked around, taking in the sights of her cozy office: a tapestry over one wall, potted plants, counseling textbooks, framed diplomas and motivational quotes. She opened a drawer to her left and pulled out a compact mirror, surveying her reflection again, the filthy collar of her blouse, after the week-long affair.

"Unreal," she whispered out loud, struggling to believe that that dreamlike chain of events had actually happened. She sat for a few moments, taking slow, even breaths, before rising to slink back across the room. Though her Accord had been the only car in the lot, she opened the door, and peeked down the hall. Satisfied the clinic was deserted, she returned to her desk.

She took another deep, drawn-out breath. When she let it out, she opened a second drawer, the one to her right, furthest from the door, furthest from the chair her patients sat in. Excavating the small, decorative box from the drawer's depths, she unlatched it, and assembled the paraphernalia. She saw, with mild amusement, that the corner of a gram-baggie she had left on her desk during her session with Nicole still sat, undisturbed.

The phone call Olive had made had not been to the number on Eddie's slip of paper, but to her own dealer, the one she'd had for the past two years. She remembered how she had feigned terror at the sight of the orange cap of the syringe in Eddie's hand. Oh, she'd been scared at first, unsure of Eddie's intentions. And she'd panicked when she'd been kidnapped in the midst of her errand, her drug run, after leaving the clinic that day, worried she'd be forced to kick dope while duct taped to a chair in a stranger's basement.

But when she realized what Eddie had planned, the comical irony of it was almost too much to bear.

Poor, pathetic Eddie. He thought he was going to teach her a lesson. Make her take her medicine. Instead, he'd relieved her of the chore of having to finance her own habit for a week's time. On her vacation, and indulging her with *fire*, as Eddie so fittingly called it, no less.

Her preparations complete, Olive expertly injected seventy cc's into the basilic vein of the underside of her arm. She supposed that her surreptitiousness in vein choice prior to being held captive had contributed to Eddie's ignorance of her true condition. That, as well as the diplomas, her overall appearance, her dress and demeanor.

She looked at the plaque on her wall and smiled.

Appearances could indeed, be deceiving.

LADY OF THE FLIES

"When the leaves turn brown and the pumpkins grin,
And the trick-or-treaters knock and say, *let me in*,
Hide your cats and your dogs, whether big or small,
'Cuz Pris-killa is coming to slay us all."

Priscila Teasdale listened to the children sing their song as they skipped through the Gourd Falls Farm pumpkin patch, and raised a sickle in one catcher's mitt-sized hand. In the other, she steadied a massive pumpkin, its stem thick as a man's forearm and connected to a substantial length of vine. She tried to steady her thoughts, but this wasn't as easy as controlling the gargantuan squash. She folded her six-foot frame at the waist, raised the blade with expert precision, and brought it down with a crack.

That's a new one, she thought with regard to the catchy

rhyme. *Was it Stu, or one of his little girlfriends, that had come up with it?* She didn't ponder the question long. People were always saying things as if she wasn't right there to hear them, forcing Priscila to conclude that she was as worthy of being seen as a street sign for a road that had washed away with last year's rains.

Of course I'm harboring skeletons in my closet. She readied another pumpkin—this one the size of a large dog—for liberation from its snaking vine. *Any woman who looks like me must have her share of skeletons, figurative or otherwise.*

For a moment, the velvety feel of the vine against her fingers reminded her of the dogs, their prickly muzzles caressing her palm. She shook her head, dispelling the corporeal memory, and focused on the present.

She brought the sickle down, only to look up and find Nathan Hitcher staring at the dilapidated barn her crew would soon convert into a labyrinth of cotton spider webs and self-playing organs. He caught her eye before she could return to her task, and gestured for her to join him.

"Mornin'," he said.

Priscila tipped an imaginary hat.

"How're the preparations comin'?"

"They're coming."

"Good, good." Nathan unscrewed an empty water bottle, spit a wad of chewing tobacco into it, and tossed it into a nearby wheelbarrow. "You've worked for my father for how long now?"

"Ten years." What she didn't say, was that it had been ten years since she'd walked out of her eleventh grade gym class and kept on walking. Walked despite the icy December air until she'd seen the sign for *Seasonal Help Wanted*; walked down the dirt path, into Hitcher's office, and right into the position of Holiday Associate. She was chopping down Christmas trees and hauling them onto the main lot before the bell would have rung for final period.

Nathan sighed. "Every October, the fate of the farm is in the hands of a bunch of idiots I wouldn't trust with a potato gun. Until now, my father has been on the scene. But this year..." He squinted in the sun.

Priscila, too, shut her eyes against the glare. She saw the black void of those sleepless nights in the weeks after Hitcher had announced the grand opening of the farm's first annual Haunted House and Corn Maze, four years prior, nights she'd watched her inevitable departure from a Gourd Falls Farm that no longer needed her as clearly as if her ceiling had morphed into a movie screen. But she'd made herself useful, mowing the mile-long path through the cornfield and installing the stage sets for the maze's main stops, and was tickled pink as the farm's newborn pigs when Hitcher had appointed her head of the *haunted construction crew*.

"I know you're quiet," Nathan said, "and I know *why* you like to keep to yourself, but I have no idea what I'm doing, and I can't let my father down. He may be sick, but it'll kill him if I blow Halloween." He wrung his hands, unblemished by the callouses that marred his father's.

Priscila bit her lower lip hard, keeping the excitement from reshaping her mouth into a smile. She was unable to prevent the warm, butterfly wings of acceptance from beating against the walls of her heart.

"I need your experience if something goes wrong. Remember last year, when those hooligans set a cornstalk on fire? And those kids that hid on the property after we closed and decked the cornfield with a twenty-four pack of toilet paper rolls?"

Of course I remember. Priscila recalled the magazine-pretty girls who would pass through, their Adonisian boyfriends feigning boredom as actors with chainsaws and scythe-brandishing grim reapers menaced them, hiding sweaty hands in letter jacket pockets. *Maybe someday I'll have someone to walk through the maze with.*

"I want to station you in the cornfield. You'd have a main base, but your primary responsibility would be to oversee the maze as a whole, so I'd want you to, well, essentially to walk the path."

Nathan put a hand on her arm and looked at her until she met his gaze. "You wouldn't have to interact with the guests. I mean that. You can yell or wave your arms to spook 'em when they walk by. And you'd have to be in costume. But like I said, it's just to make sure there's no funny business and that everyone gets through this season unscathed, the farm included." Nathan's eyebrows furrowed with uncertainty. "It's just an idea. If you're not up for it, you can tell me. What do you think?"

Priscila hesitated, and Nathan quickly continued, "Look, I know what people say about you. So if you're unsure because—"

"You mean if I'm unsure because they say that my farmhouse is a dead ringer for the one from the *Texas Chainsaw* movies? Or because people can't decide if I'm a serial killer with dead bodies to hide or a child molester with stacks of pornography?"

Nathan flinched. "I'm sorry. I didn't mean to suggest that the things people say shouldn't bother you. It's just that, well, what I'm trying to say is... everyone knows that it was parvo that killed your dogs, not you. You have to stop beating yourself up. Who could have known it would spread so fast?"

While Nathan stammered, Priscila remembered the feel of her arms wrapped around the neck of her last, beloved dog. *But I did kill one of them,* she thought. *At least, I think I did...*

After the contagion had left her with a single surviving female, Priscila had grown ill herself. One morning, having missed a week of work, delirious and roiling in fever-soaked sheets, she awoke on the floor on top of the motionless animal, the flies buzzing mercilessly. She hadn't been sure if the dog had been sick after all or if she had smothered the pitiable thing in the night.

Priscila shook the thought away, recalling instead the way kindly old Mr. Hitcher had given her a job all those years ago with hardly a question asked. This, coupled with the way Nathan had sought her out, the way he was, despite his obliviousness to the abuse she regularly endured, really *seeing* her...

Priscila felt needed for the first time since the dogs. She replied, "Whatever you need me to do."

Nathan still looked tentative. "Are you sure? I need you to be really sure. I don't want you to feel like you're taking on too much responsibility. Not after—"

"I can do it."

Nathan grinned, and pumped his fist. "Great. We'll make this work, Priscila. I know we will."

Priscila blushed and studied her dust-coated hands. In the wake of her excitement, the tune of the *Pris-killa* ditty faded from her mind.

The rest of the day was experienced in high-definition for all her private glee. After Priscila reshaped the path through the cornfield, she steered toward the storage shed to return the John Deere. As she exited the shed's side door, she collided head-on with a short, dark-haired man.

She refrained from reaching out to right him, and was relieved when the man found his footing himself. Priscila waited for him to curse and hurl accusations, but when she looked up, the man—out of place in the dust and hayseed in his button-down shirt and shiny shoes—was smiling.

"I think I'm lost," he said sheepishly. "I wanted to buy tickets for the maze thing this weekend for me and my friends."

Priscila averted her eyes from that smile. Friends was not a word to which she could lay claim.

The man shifted his weight from one foot to the other. "Can you point me in the direction of the ticket counter?"

Priscila froze. *Would a normal person speak the words? Or should I walk him to the farm stand? Do I want to be that visible for such a prolonged period of time?*

Them's just people, she heard the voice of Mr. Hitcher say. *No sense bein' a'scared of 'em. Ask 'em their name and figure out how to give 'em what they want.*

"What's your name?" she managed.

"Mike Golding."

He reached out to shake her hand, but Priscila pretended she hadn't seen, and was moving quickly toward the shop. "It's right this way," she whispered.

When she'd made it to the barn that functioned as both ticket counter and gift shop, she exhaled an audible sigh of relief.

Mike turned and gestured toward the barn. "Thanks. I could get lost in a paper bag. Of course my buddies sent me to get the tickets, when I'm the only one that hasn't been here before. Will you be here on Opening Night?"

"Yes. Overseeing the maze." The words felt foreign on her tongue, but sweet too, like candy corn.

"Awesome, maybe I'll see you Sunday night. Thanks again." This time his smile was wide enough for Priscila to notice dimples in both cheeks. He pushed open the door, and disappeared.

"Awesome," Priscila whispered to herself. Her scalp tingled. A strange giddiness flooded her insides.

At five, she crossed the dusty parking lot, tired, but content. The foliage seemed to transcend mere oranges and yellows in its brilliance, and the laughter of the other farm workers bothered her not. *What an odd feeling,* she thought. *Contentment.*

Priscila heaved her aching body into the front seat of her pickup truck. Upon rolling down the window to enjoy the crisp autumn air, she was surprised to hear someone call her name.

"Priscila, hey!" Stu Perkins was slouched in the front seat of his own pickup a few spots over. That season's girlfriend sat beside him, her expression sour.

Priscila raised a hand in greeting.

"I hear you're going to be the new Lord Commander of Castle Gourd Falls."

Priscila stared. The words made no sense to her strung together as they'd been.

"Sorry, TV show reference." Stu struggled to see past his girlfriend's hunched shoulders as she stifled a cascade of laughter. "I meant that you're going to actually be taking part in the haunted stuff this year. Nathan told us that on maze nights, you're the boss and he'd fire anyone that didn't listen to you."

Priscila shrugged, but she studied Stu's face. *He seems to think me worthy of his attention for having been given this responsibility.* "Nathan wants things to run smoothly," was all she said.

"We have a lot of fun every October." Stu started his truck. His girlfriend was examining her manicure, and missed Stu's wink. "I think it's cool you're going to be more involved."

With that, he drove off. Within seconds, the interaction began to feel like the remnants of an elaborate daydream.

Adding into account the conversations with Nathan and Mike Golding, Priscila felt even less certain of her sanity. *It had been real*, she told herself. *All three interactions had been real.*

She drove home, less convinced of her pickup's tires spinning along the road than she was of floating to her destination on a cloud of euphoria.

—

138

She left her boots on the mat inside the door and moved like a cat through the pitch-dark foyer. Priscila had lived in the farmhouse since she was born, and had only become more accustomed to its creaking boards and oversized rooms since her father had left her the ten-acre property upon his death a decade earlier.

She rummaged through a kitchen cabinet until she found a pan, took a spatula from a drawer, and hummed as she slipped the chicken potpie she'd made that weekend into the oven.

When the food was hot, and after Priscila had watched the filth of the farm wash down the shower drain, she took her dinner and a bottle of beer and headed for the living room. She had to navigate around a maze-like tunnel at the center of the hall, and she pulled a cord attached to a piece of plywood, cut to match the width of the doorway, to gain access.

Priscila placed her dinner on the coffee table and sifted through a stack of magazines. She chose a recent issue of *Farm & Fireside*, but knocked the stack with her arm as she turned, sending half the pile falling.

The cover of one of the magazines caught her eye. With the caution of someone approaching a poisonous snake, Priscila picked up a months old issue of *Family Dog*, the American Kennel Club-issued periodical, with thumb and forefinger. The warming beer and cooling dinner faded from mind and she sank into her worn leather armchair to examine the vivid photo on the front.

A sturdy, stoic Rottweiler stood in a field of lush green grass, its wide mouth seeming to grin, its substantial muscles rippling beneath a black-and-mahogany coat. Priscila ran a finger along the outline of the handsome creature. Before she could blink it away, a tear fell from one cornflower blue eye and splattered against the glossy stock.

No. Not tonight. Priscila tore the cover from the magazine, crumpled it into a ball, and tossed into the fireplace. An echo came, the words her father had spoken the day her uncle had pulled up to the Teasdale farm with a flatbed full of plump, two-toned puppies: *You think Priscila will do any better connecting with the other kids if her only companion becomes a hundred-and-fifty pound mass of teeth and drool and muscle?*

Priscila pressed her hands to her ears. She would hear no more.

She stood and walked her untouched potpie back into the kitchen, where she deposited it into the sink. She regarded the paint-chipped lockbox on the counter. After her father died, joining the mother who had abandoned Priscila at birth, it was in this box that she'd kept the money she'd saved. It took eight months to afford male and female Rottweilers of suitable breeding.

Leaving the kitchen, she moved to a room at the front of the farmhouse. Moonlight filtered through trees slowly shedding their leaves, and cast shadows on the floor, in which Priscila could just make out the ghosts of eight puppies. Priscila had assisted in dozens of births, puppies that went first to neighbors, then to visitors of Gourd Falls Farm Hitcher had sent her way.

She would not go to the back of the house, to the spacious, many-windowed room where the corpses of flies still littered the floor and stacks of metal crates and rows of surgical tables gleamed in the dark. *All remaining tours of this haunted house have been cancelled until further notice,* she thought, and forced a chuckle, a smile for the dogs that had actually made it. She maneuvered through the hall, still rigged to accommodate the various litters at various stages of development, and climbed the stairs to her father's old bedroom, hers now, though it remained unchanged.

From the window, Priscila could see rows of makeshift grave markers in the field.

Remember what happened when you aspired for more than you deserved?

But another voice, buoyed by the good day she'd had, by the feeling that she was getting a second chance, spoke back: *This will be different. This time, you will make things work.*

She thought of Stu Perkins—*I think it's cool that you're going to be more involved*—and the final sharp edges of her memories smoothed. She climbed into bed.

The ticking of the clock convinced her to close her eyes.

She switched off the lamp.

Tonight, she would not need it to combat the darkness of her thoughts.

—

The first night Priscila was to oversee the corn maze, the moon was full and the temperature was in the forties. On her way to find Nathan, she overheard Stu's girlfriend complaining bitterly, outraged that the thin fabric of her deranged nurse costume wouldn't offer even the slightest protection against the cold.

When the younger Hitcher saw Priscila approaching, his

expression melted into one of relief. "Priscila, thank God. Follow me."

In the storage shed, she watched him root around in a large cardboard box, muttering to himself. "Aha," he said, turning to hide something behind his back. "You ready?"

Priscila uncrossed her arms from over her chest.

The mask that Nathan revealed was a grotesque, exquisite model of a slightly-larger-than-average pig's head. The pointed, pink ears had been preserved with some sort of shellac, and the eyeholes were red-rimmed, as if the flesh had only recently been pared away from muscle. Greasy black hair hung down to the snout, and its mouth had been stitched shut with thick black cord.

"What do you think?" Nathan asked.

Priscila stared.

Revulsion clashing with curiosity, she ran her fingers along one side of the sloped face. "It looks so real." Her chest tightened at her mind's realization that the frozen face of death could appear so similar across species, but relaxed when she imagined Stu's reaction to the mask's badassery.

"About that. Remember how I told you you'd have a home base somewhere along the path? I wanted you to have realistic props, in case you were keen on scaring people after all, and, well, today was slaughter day..."

Priscila pinched the mask now, getting a feel for how it yielded beneath the pressure of her fingers. "You... carved it." She was regarding Nathan's handiwork thoughtfully. "You made it yourself."

"Yeah." Nathan looked embarrassed. "Is that weird?"

"It's really cool." Priscila took the mask from him. She was surprised by how heavy it was in her hands.

She pried her eyes from her gift to find Nathan studying her. "What's wrong?" she asked.

"How long has it been since you've had a night this full of human interaction? Have you done anything this taxing since... well, since the dogs? Are you sure you're ready for this?"

Priscila reddened. "Please don't ask me again. I told you I'd be fine. You're making me feel like a freak."

"I'm sorry." Nathan rifled through the box again, anxious to move past his blunder. "The other stuff you can take or leave, but I thought it'd go good with the mask." He unearthed a rubber butcher's apron, then retrieved a bucket from the corner of the storage shed and set it down between them.

He checked the time; Priscila felt something tug in her chest as she recognized Mr. Hitcher's pocket watch. "I should get a move on," he said. "There are a million things to do and only a half hour 'til we open the gate."

He pushed the bucket across the gritty floor with the toe of his boot. "There's a workbench on concrete blocks halfway through the trail. That's your spot. Like I said, it was slaughter day, so why let these go to waste?"

Touched that Nathan had thought of her, Priscila peered inside the bucket, where extraneous pig parts—organs, a curly-Q tail, and four large hooves—marinated in blackish blood.

"You can use them tonight, but since our grand opening fell on a Sunday, I'll either have to get you some rubber replacements before Friday, or..." He shrugged, the gesture unexpectedly charming. "We'll have to slaughter another pig next week, won't we?"

A pleasant heat rose to her cheeks at the reference to her continued involvement with the corn maze.

He jostled her good-naturedly as he exited the shed, and Priscila jerked to keep the rubber apron from slipping from her elbow. "I'm counting on you," he called over his shoulder. "But it won't kill you to have a little fun either."

———

It took her longer than she'd anticipated to reach the workbench, and she wasted no time in spreading the contents of her bucket across it. She fastened a tool belt around her waist, replete with flashlight, walkie-talkie, penknife, and a small first aid kit, and donned the apron over it. She placed the mask on the ground beside the cinderblocks and listened to the rustling of the cornstalks, wondering how, exactly, she had come to be at this juncture.

She was about to radio Nathan, tell him thank you, that she never thought she'd appreciate the opportunity to shroud herself in the corpse of a pig and menace teenagers with bloody hooves, when the pounding of footsteps reached her ears. Before she could push-to-talk, a towering werewolf with blazing red eyes darted into the clearing.

It raised its snout to the moon and howled, then stalked toward her on elongated, sharp-clawed feet. Priscila opened her mouth, but did not speak. The werewolf sniffed in her direction, lifting its paws to either side of its face. When the mask had been lowered, Stu Perkins looked back at her, grinning lopsidedly. "You almost ready? I ran here from the entry point. Alex is going to let people in any minute. Where's the rest of your costume?"

Priscila let her gaze fall to her own mask. She lifted it slowly, gauging Stu's reaction before bringing it down over her face.

"Ho-ly shit!" She heard Stu as if from underwater. "You look... awesome! That mask is terrifying."

Beneath her new face, Priscila smiled. So that Stu would know she'd heard, she gave him a thumbs-up.

A screech funneled through the cornstalks, devolving into peals of laughter.

"I should go," Stu said.

Priscila nodded. From the expression on his face, she could tell that movement undertaken while wearing the mask had a mesmerizing, paralyzing effect, away from which the onlooker couldn't turn.

"One more thing," Stu said. His eyes went to the ground. "I didn't invite you in the past because you weren't really part of the Halloween crew, and it didn't seem like you'd have wanted to come anyway, but every year, on opening night, I throw a party back at my place."

Of course I'd have wanted to come, but how could I have told you that when I've never been able to articulate anything, let alone the desire to be around other people, Priscila thought wildly. *But I'll come now! Of course I'll come now.*

"Everyone wears their costumes," Stu continued. Though he'd apparently suppressed his guilty conscience enough to lift his gaze from the ground, he'd managed to raise his eyes only to the level of Priscila's chest. "Nathan lets the concession girls bring a bunch of food and we kick back and celebrate the start of another October."

The laughter and shouting grew closer, and Stu raised the werewolf mask, ready to run. "Will you come?" he asked. His eyes seemed to encompass six years' worth of remorse.

I forgive you, she thought. *You're bossy girlfriends might have convinced you to be mean to me in the past, but I forgive you because you want to make it up to me now.*

"Will you?" Stu repeated.

"Yes," she whispered.

A strand of the greasy black wig fell into her line of vision. When she'd brushed it back, Stu was gone. Priscila was alone, but she didn't mind.

Tonight would not be a night for being alone.

—

Only once in the course of Opening Night did Priscila experience a twinge of her usual invisibility. She'd been informed over the walkie-talkie that the approaching group spouting profanities and trying to scare the female actors were the men that Alex had very nearly not let through in the first place, their levels of intoxication bordering on obscene.

Priscila steadied her breathing as she listened to the savages advance. Despite the chill and the late hour, a small swarm of flies had abandoned the fertilized fields for Priscila's sticky banquet. They buzzed around her while the men piled into the clearing. Right away, Priscila recognized Mike Golding.

"Wh—what... the hell?" One of Mike's friends had caught sight of her.

She saw herself standing beside the tableau of gristle and

146

blood as they would see her: a six-foot tall pig woman with blood-tinged flesh and a dead gaze issuing forth from deep-socketed eyes, engulfed by the cloying odor of rust and adrenalized fear. The star of the freak show.

Priscila grimaced. In response, she swore she felt the mask's snout twitch.

Mike slipped a flask from his pocket. Eyes on Priscila, he unscrewed its lid.

They come here to be scared. I'm in costume, not a freak, and they come here to be scared. Maybe Mike will remember me, think I'm cool for freaking out his friends.

As she contemplated this, she sensed the men's attention waning. They were getting ready to move on, to the next section of the maze. Intent on doing something drastic, on being seen, she rushed at them on feet more deft than her own. Her lips contorted, producing an infernal roar. One hand let fly a chunk of gallbladder as she pumped her arms; a rope of the slaughtered pig's large intestine was flung from the other.

Mike's eyes widened and he cried out. He tried to bolt, caught his foot in a divot in the dusty ground, and stumbled. He scuttled backward, desperate to retreat from the advancing monster. Priscila halted two feet from the men and watched as Mike pushed himself up. On one knee, he turned a face full of embarrassed hatred up to Priscila's masked one.

"Here," Mike's friend said, reaching down to help Mike to his feet. Mike knocked the hand away.

Dread pooled in Priscila's gut like bad food.

"Let's get out of here." The friend attempted to herd the

group back toward the cornfield, but Mike remained rooted in place.

"No. This bitch took a cheap shot. We have to make her pay." His eyes glittered in the moonlight. "Kill the pig," he said. "Cut her throat. Spill her blood."

Priscila flexed her fingers. *Tonight was supposed to be a good night. A night I could remember for interacting with friends, for feeling included. Tonight wasn't supposed to be a night for ugliness.*

She had never had a therapist, but a dog trainer had once told her to take a single, calming breath before disciplining the puppies. She did that now, sick at how poorly her attempt at being noticed had gone over, at her misjudgment of how Mike would react to being scared.

"Seriously, Mike, the quicker we get to the end of this thing, the quicker we get back to the bar."

Mike held the mask's gaze, his lip curled. Finally, he allowed one side of the sneer to lift into a sinister smile. "Yeah. Okay. Let's go." He followed his friends through a slit in the stalks, his eyes flicking to hers for a last, cold look before he disappeared into the dark.

His angry, taunting voice came to her on the wind: "Next time, we kill the pig."

—

When the last haunted house-patron had exited the barn, and Priscila had cleared the maze, scooped her props back into the bucket, and removed her second skin, it occurred to her to wonder if Stu would have her follow him to the party, or offer her a ride.

I bet he'll give me a ride. We'll talk about how Opening Night went, and then we'll—

She was about to step from between wispy, shifting stalks, when a voice, shrill and unhappy, cut through the night.

"What do you mean, you invited her? Are you insane? Tell her she can't come!"

Priscila froze. Her eyes stung at the malice in Stu's girlfriend's voice.

"She's part of the crew now, what difference does it make?"

Priscila nearly dropped the mask, sweat causing her to lose her grip, but she caught it before it could hit the ground and give her location away.

"Let's leave! Then she won't know how to get there."

Priscila waited for Stu to refuse, to suggest that maybe *she* should leave. But Stu only sighed.

"Please," the girl pleaded.

The tone was so childish, so pained, much like...

Priscila heard herself whisper, so pitifully it seemed not to have come from her own lips: *please*. And perhaps she hadn't uttered it. Perhaps it was only a memory...

Another set of footsteps crunched through the leaves.

"Nathan," the girl whined. Priscila had never learned her name. "Can you please tell Stu he can't have Pris-killa at the party tonight? It'll be weird for everyone there."

"You invited Priscila?" There was surprise in Nathan's voice. "I don't know if that's such a good idea."

Priscila swallowed the lump in her throat.

Under the weight of their judgement, Stu sighed again. "Fine. You guys are probably right." He snorted. "I mean,

God forbid she really is a murderous psychopath and someone finds us all tomorrow morning, dead as her fucking dogs. Speaking of fucking dogs, she probably did fuck them, and that's how they all croaked. Let's go before she comes out of the maze."

Priscila's devastation was like breathing too close to a fire; the acuteness of it instigated choking.

She sat on the cold earth, chewing on a husk and stroking the smooth flesh of a pig that, like her, had been alive only that morning. She felt carved out, as empty as the grinning jack-o'-lanterns that welcomed visitors to Gourd Falls. When she was sure the farm was vacant, she struggled to her feet.

They left me. They left me without a second thought, and all I'd wanted was one thing to call my own. My own dog. A livelihood. A fulfilling relationship with a co-worker. A friend.

She walked through the silent farm grounds. The bucket of pig parts swung from one hand, while the mask lolled gently from the other.

And the tears Priscila cried cut through the tinge of blood staining her cheeks like razors drawn through tender flesh.

—

Her headlights cut through the fog, sunrays trying to penetrate too-deep water, and she drove slowly, not caring if she ever made it home. She had crested the top of Rabbit Run Road when she saw the cherry red Range Rover. The smoke billowing from beneath the hood was thick even in the impenetrable fog, and the tree the driver had barreled into was stark in the up-close beam of its only working headlight.

Priscila pulled up beside the wreck. She climbed out and

was at the driver's side door in four long strides, more excited now than she'd been at any point policing the maze.

Either the driver's window had been down, or it had shattered so completely that not a single shard remained in its frame, impossible to determine in conjunction with the demolished windshield. An arm hung from the open window, the hand wedged between the accordioned front bumper severed from the wrist but for the thinnest rope of muscle.

Priscila reached out and touched the man's wrist, an inch above the injury. The traumatized flesh reminded her of her mask. The man stirred, moaned. When he lifted his head and locked eyes with Priscila, she heard the echo of his voice coming to her in the cornfield: "Kill the pig," he had chanted. "Cut her throat."

My piglets have come home to sty.

"Help."

The word was raspy, reminded her of the skitter of paw pads on the farmhouse floor. Priscila turned and walked back to her truck.

Mike called after her, panicked.

She returned only seconds later, the pig mask covering her face. Mike whimpered. In those unfocused eyes, Priscila saw the liquid brown ones of her Rottweiler, cataracted in death and the glare of the morning sun.

Priscila reached out. She took the man's wrist in one large hand and pressed the other against the battered metal.

She pulled.

In her truck, Mike regained consciousness only once. "Hospital," he croaked. He held his arm to his chest, the stump wrapped in a dirty swatch of burlap.

The pig woman nodded.

—

He did not wake until many nights later and by then, the flies had descended upon the farmhouse like a plague. The room was a series of twists and turns, a maze of passages made from wood and metal and sheetrock. At the far end of the labyrinth was a door, outside which was a night lit only by the moon.

The door slid open and a harrowing figure in a rubber butcher's apron emerged. Its face was a macabre impossibility, a dripping candle of waxen horror, half-melted flesh ripped from some fever dreamed up in Hell. The rotting flesh moved in a writhing kaleidoscope, animated by the bodies of hundreds upon hundreds of flies. More flies circled its ears; they crawled in and out of its sunken, sodden eyes.

The man in the dog crate went to crawl from his prison. He stopped when his hand clanked wrongly on the bars. He directed his attention downward, saw the hoof that replaced his hand. Shock of a sort unable to be adequately expressed suffused his pallid face.

"I had to," the pig said. The gilt pig. Madame Pig. Madame Piggy. "And I had to do them all to make it even."

The man began to convulse, beholding his hoof-hands, hoof-feet, the Frankensteinian stitches, red-raw flesh, white, bloodless skin that frayed along the edges.

"Why?" The one discernible word he managed.

A fly flew into his open mouth, crawled across his swollen tongue. Priscila, in her pig mask, looked out across the shadow-ridden farm, the buzzing of the flies like an unseen spacecraft forming crop circles in the fields.

Sensing motion, a porch light kicked on.

"I tried for too much. I see that now. I tried to hold onto things I'd never have been able to keep. I'm content with the things that are willing to come to me. The flies, for one. They don't require much. And you."

The man's cries turned into squeals of fear. "Beast!" he choked out.

Priscila rubbed her gloved hands together.

"Maybe there is a beast... and maybe it's only us. Either way, you are here. Everyone wants to be Lord or Lady of something. If I must settle for you, than I thought I should make us as similar as possible. You have me, in all that makes me invisible, unworthy of connection. And I have you, in all that makes you incomplete. A freak."

It felt good to talk. If felt good to have someone listen.

Methodically, Mike rapped his hooves against the bars. The sound was like the beating of a steel drum.

"And the flies. I mustn't forget about the flies. They visited me once before, and how ungrateful I was then."

She turned to him. She had cut the stitches at the pig's mouth, so it appeared that even with the mask on, Priscila was smiling. The porch light was positioned so that the mask's holes seemed to glow from within.

Her captive tried to scramble backward, fear driving him to panic. "Your face!" he screamed. "What is wrong with your face?"

"What *is* a face?" Priscila asked. "What is anything, really?"

And she joined him in the pounding of the bars.

THE GIRL WHO LOVED BRUCE CAMPBELL

No Bottom Pond might have had a bottom, but as far as the three clammy and restless individuals that sat in the idling car by its banks knew, it very well might not. The cold sweats and body aches would not assail them for much longer; the lankier of the two males divvied up the wax baggies of brown powder, and each in turn began their own sacred ritual of preparation. It took only seconds for the first of the three to realize a key element was missing from their assorted paraphernalia.

"Damn," the stocky male said. "Does anyone have a water bottle?"

There was no reply as each of the three checked the space around their feet, and the nearest cup holder.

"Now what?" the lone female asked. "We can't hit a gas station. We need to stay off the roads for a while; someone may have seen us leave that house."

There was murmured agreement from the two men, followed by a morose silence. The lanky man broke the quiet with a snort of derision.

"This shit's fried our brains," he said. "We're sitting next to a lake, complaining about not having any water to shoot up with."

"It's not a lake, it's a pond," the woman said.

"Technically, it's not even a pond. It's an estuary. And we can't use that water because it's brackish." The stouter man sounded matter-of-fact.

"What's brackish mean? That it's dirty? Please, I've seen you use water from the tank of a gas station toilet, dirty should be the least of your worries." This, from the woman.

"No, not dirty, *brackish*. It means it's half freshwater, half salt. We can't shoot that, it might mess with our bodies' electrolyte levels or something." Now the stocky man sounded less sure of himself.

The lanky man opened the car door. He reached for an empty Dunkin Donuts cup discarded on the floor of the passenger seat, removed the lid, and looked suspiciously into its depths. Shrugging, he started for the pond's weedy shore.

"I didn't get away with a B&E and buy dope from the shadiest dealer in town to let a little saltwater stop me. It's only *half* salt anyways," he called over his shoulder.

The woman and the stout man watched him creep toward the water's edge. He folded his tall frame in half and scooped a cupful of water into the Styrofoam. He did this in the light of a moon so close it seemed to be perched atop the hill that loomed over No Bottom Pond, a luminous cherry bedecking a black forest cake.

The first full moon to rise on Christmas in forty years had occurred the night before. "A Christmas miracle," the woman had said sarcastically as they listened to a radio talk show host lament the previous night's fog cover on their way to Shore Road, and the house they'd been casing most of the past week. The upscale home had yielded extensive reserves of jewelry, cash, and three guns. There'd been a safe, but they had no use for a safe. They only took what they could trade quickly and easily to their dealer, and their dealer had no interest in safes.

The lunar display of December twenty-sixth happened to be free from a smothering blanket of fog. As the woman watched the tall man return, she noticed that in the bright moonlight, the water's surface had a strange sparkle to it, was almost phosphorescent in the gleam. Parts of the pond were the shiny, black, oil-slick of water-in-moonlight she'd expect. Having spent her whole life in the seaside town, she'd seen water undulating under the moon enough times for the sight to be commonplace, but No Bottom Pond was greenish in its radiance, and did not steam so much as gurgle, like the stew in a witch's cauldron.

She forgot her inquisitiveness over the appearance of the water when the passenger door slammed shut. Three syringe tips plunged greedily into the captured pond water, transporting water from cup to three waiting spoons. Mysticism, Rhode Island was a small town, and the population was reduced by half in the winter. The heroin dealers had been tapped into the same pipelines in and out of the closest major cities for decades; the three longtime users expected the same cut and purity of dope they'd had on the previous day, and on the occasion of their first use.

Subsequently, no lighter flicked on to form dancing shadows on the car walls, no Butane-fueled flame burned prospective toxins out of the contents of their spoons. They each shot up, one, two, three, and each fell into that first nod of euphoria, a scarecrow short of Dorothy and her comrades in the poppy field.

At the same time that legions of fish were rising to the vaporous surface of No Bottom Pond, dead and already beginning to putrefy, small boils popped up under the skin of the three beings in the car. The tall man thought he'd injected a hot shot, while the woman jerked out of her nod in wild agitation to inspect the tip of her needle, convinced she'd given herself cotton fever by neglecting to free the point from Q-tip remnants. Both of them were wrong.

The mutations occurred quickly and the changes were profound. When the transformation was complete, the three beings were no longer satisfied with the heroin that flowed through their veins. They were hungry in a way that made every torturous withdrawal symptom or harrowing mental craving of the past seem like a petty annoyance, a minor itch that could go without being scratched.

—

Two hours earlier, a local scientist named Craig Silas stood on a dip of Watch Hill Road, a dark silhouette overlooking the river that rushed into No Bottom Pond. Craig worked at a nearby pharmaceutical company, and the previous year had snuck a project home to his basement laboratory to continue his work free from the oversight and ethical regulations of his employer.

In the wake of a countrywide opiate epidemic, Big Pharma had sufficient incentive to develop an opioid-free painkiller, eliminating the potential for abuse and addiction. Craig had stumbled onto an unanticipated side effect of the chemical compound he'd been studying, and upon bringing his research home, further unlocked the potential of the drug. Characteristics included superhuman strength, laser-point focus, and a complete inability to feel pain. Craig spent weeks hypothesizing on the drug's limitless prospects, until he'd descended the basement stairs one morning to find one of the pink-eyed lab rats feasting on his cage-mates' brains. With every possibility of experiencing pain eliminated, the rats' behavior had morphed into something much more ominous... and much more deadly.

After driving up and down the streets of Mysticism with the concoction swishing around a large vat in his trunk, Craig noticed that the adjacent river ran beneath the road and into a wide inlet. Theorizing that the body of water before him was the equivalent of a dead end street, he pulled onto the narrow shoulder and muscled the vat onto the guardrail before another car could appear. Craig Silas had left No Bottom Pond ten miles behind him by the time his miracle drug had seeped into the pond's ecosystem, and was home in his favorite armchair with his feet up by the time the first transformations began to occur.

—

Sophisticated cognition already reduced to animalistic compulsion, the three addicts, who had become fiends of a different nature, were barely able to recall the chain of events that had led them to their last high, brought to the utmost intensity by the unorthodox mixture of heroin and pond-dispersed, opiate-free analgesic. But they were able to recall enough to know what they needed to do to feed the hunger that gnawed at their insides like so many of Silas' lab rats. And so they began to move.

—

Kartya watched the spray of blood waterfall through the front door of the cabin, and grabbed Kit's arm.

"That... was... awesome!" she cheered, the arm-grabbing escalating to arm-slapping. She turned to face her boyfriend. "How much time is left?"

"Kar, just watch, I'm not messing with it again. It's thirty minutes long, like all the other episodes."

This appeased Kartya enough to watch the last ten minutes in silence. She twirled a ringlet of cherry-coke-colored hair around blood-red fingernails. When the show was over, she turned to Kit again, eager to hear his opinion on the latest installment.

"Well," Kit said, "they definitely set us up for an epic showdown at the cabin."

"Agreed! I wish there was more than ten episodes. That was a good one though. Buckets of blood!" A mischievous smile turned up the corners of her lips.

"Twisted, gory, and hilarious," Kit said. "That dead cop put her fists through the campers' skulls, and turned them into corpse puppets!"

"Let's be serious, most of the other characters only exist to compliment Ash. To give the directors a springboard for his one-liners and so that we can see some different weapons brandished against the Deadites. It can't all be about Ash's chainsaw arm and Boomstick." She mimed obliterating Kit with a shotgun blast to the face.

"Also," she continued, "did I tell you that Ash, err, sorry, Bruce Campbell, wrote an autobiography a few years back... called *If Chins Could Kill?*"

Kit gave her a look that conveyed both incredulity and reverence, and broke into a hearty chuckle, no doubt visualizing the B-list movie actor's signature square chin.

"That's amazing. You need to get that book." He gestured to two bookshelves flanking the television, which still rolled the blood-splattered credits for the show.

Kartya nodded with enthusiasm but did not turn to regard the bookshelves, pointing instead to the two Vinyl Pop characters facing off from their respective posts atop surround sound speakers. The plastic Ash and *Army of Darkness* Deadite had been Christmas gifts from her mother the previous morning. Though she didn't share her daughter's love for horror, Kartya's mother knew Kartya and Kit harbored a cultish enthusiasm for Ash, and all things *Evil Dead*, from the campy originals to the 2013 remake, and now, the television series. She had wrapped the figurines knowing it would bring appreciative smiles to their faces.

"Instead of that speaker, a hardcover copy of *If Chins*

Could Kill could be mini-Ash's battleground in the fight against evil," Kartya said.

Kit smiled and got to his feet.

"You're cute, babe. I love that you love blood and guts as much as I do." Kit stretched his six-foot-three frame toward the ceiling and let out a groan. "But the party's over. I have to get to work."

"I can't believe you agreed to work the night after Christmas." She tried to pout, but a yawn claimed her features instead. "Although to be honest, you won't miss much. I'm beat, and will be asleep fifteen minutes after you leave."

As Kit dragged himself up the stairs to change, Kartya heard a muffled chime, and realized she was sitting on her phone. A preview of the text message scrolled across the screen. Kartya's friend Laura had written: *Better lock your door…*

Laura did well as an emergency room nurse, working as an independent contractor in different hospitals from Hartford to Boston. She vacationed often, and had returned that morning from her fourth trip to St. John since the year began. Kartya thumbed at the screen until she could see the rest of the message. In its entirety, it read: *Better lock your door… because my house got broken into.*

A fat worm of fear speared itself between the layers of Kartya's intestines. There had been numerous reports of break-ins in Mysticism over the last month, and Laura lived less than a mile from the riverfront home Kartya and Kit rented. Her fingers jerking in furious spasms, Kartya texted Laura back: *Were you home? Are you okay? What did they take?*

As she waited for Laura's reply, Kit trudged back down the stairs. He was able to read the worry on her face with a single glance.

"What is it?"

"Laura and Seth's house got broken into. I asked her what they took and if they were home. She hasn't answered me yet."

The concern on Kit's face mixed with anger. With a grim head shake, he reached out to pull her off the couch.

"This isn't happening. No way they switch me to the night shift a month before the worst string of burglaries this town's ever seen. Follow me."

"Why? Where are we going?" Kartya's attention was split between his grip on her forearm and her phone announcing a newly-arrived message.

Kit gestured up the stairs, but let go of her so she could navigate to her text message app. She read silently, her brow creased, then raised her eyes to meet Kit's.

"She said they were out getting drinks and they came home to a broken window in the living room. They'd been on vacation for the past week so someone obviously anticipated an empty house. They took jewelry, cash, some other valuables..." Kartya tried to trail off effectively, as if this was the extent of stolen goods.

"And? What else?" When she didn't answer, he said, "What else did they take, Kartya?"

"Three guns were missing," she said, knowing this information would fan Kit's anger and apprehension into a full-blown blaze.

Motivated anew, Kit took her hand and resumed their

ascent. In the guest bedroom, he retrieved a lockbox from an opaque-fronted entertainment stand.

"I would never forgive myself if something happened to you. I know you're going to protest, but agree to it for my sake." He pulled a handgun from the box and spun the chamber, counting bullets.

"Kit," Kartya objected.

"Please, come here so I can give you a quick refresher on how to..."

"Kit—" She was about to insist on an end to this ridiculous conversation. Instead, Kartya sighed and took the gun from Kit's hands, showing him that she remembered how to wield the weapon properly, cocking the hammer and adopting a shooter's stance.

"You've dragged me to the range a hundred times. I know what I'm doing well enough to defend myself if it came to it."

Kit nodded, but he was distracted. She cleared the chamber and handed the gun back to Kit. Spinning on her heel for the hall, she stopped short when she heard the scrape of something much larger being liberated from the closet.

Without turning, she said, "Kit, I do *not* need the shotgun to be within arm's reach when I go to bed tonight."

Torn between Kartya's obvious intention to refuse the shotgun and his need to be assured of her safety, Kit placed the shotgun on top of the stand.

"Fine," he said, "but I'm leaving it here, just in case. The revolver is going on your nightstand, and that's not open for discussion."

"Fine," Kartya said, her belief that the house was

impregnable, that the probability of burglars targeting their quiet, one-acre lot over any other in town causing her to grow bored with the conversation. "Drive safe please, and try to have a good night at work."

Kartya let Kit lead her into their bedroom, saying nothing as he placed the revolver on a paperback, two feet from where she was to lay her head upon the pillow. He kissed her goodnight and turned off the bedside lamp. Kartya listened to his footsteps on the stairs as she nestled beneath the covers. She had overblown her prediction: it took far less than fifteen minutes after Kit's departure for Kartya to fall asleep.

—

A noise woke her, what sounded like the skeletal finger of a winter-dead tree tapping on a window. She sat up, disoriented. Had Kit forgotten something, perhaps his badge, or the food he'd packed to eat on his break? She groped for her cell, found the button to illuminate the screen. Ten forty-five. Kit would be forty-five minutes into an hour-long commute, so it wouldn't be him tapping. She strained to catch the sound again, but it had stopped. Kartya sunk down onto the pillow, drawing the comforter up to her neck, then groaned. She flung the comforter back, forcing herself to bear the cold trek to the bathroom before returning to sleep. Halfway there, the tapping began again.

Kartya froze. There in the hallway, equally removed from both the revolver and the shotgun Kit had set out for her protection, vulnerable in her bare feet, with full bladder and panic fluttering in her brain like a moth inside a lantern, the details of the nearby break-in came roaring back, having been temporarily stolen by the fugue of sleep.

Rooted in paralysis, her rational mind attempted to quell her fears, shuffling through a series of scenarios from the ever-popular home-alone-with-an-overactive-imagination script: *It's nothing... it's just the wind... the house is settling... there's a perfectly reasonable explanation for this...* Grasping at these possibilities with the same tenacity as a drowning swimmer flailing for a rescue buoy, she started down the stairs in the dark.

Kartya's bare feet sunk into the shag carpet as she crossed the living room to the big picture window on the right. Cursing the peaks and gables of the roofline for preventing the moon from aiding her in her endeavor, she changed direction, moving from the window to the front door, whacking her hip on the corner of the heavy oak desk along the way, and switched on the outdoor floodlights.

Giving the desk a wider berth, she crept back to the right, so focused on the grate-free expanse of the window that she did not see the shadow stretched across the ground in front of her.

The Kandarian Demon had possessed a hapless civilian and turned them into a Deadite. At least, this was the only explanation that occurred to Kartya when she came face-to-face with the diseased-looking monstrosity separated from her by only half an inch of glass. For one breathless moment, Kartya thought she was dreaming, or perhaps had slipped on the stairs and knocked herself out, and was now suffering some trauma-induced hallucination. The demon-thing cocked its head to one side, emitted a guttural chuffing noise, and Kartya knew that somehow, what she was seeing was real.

She might have stood staring into the black pits of the creature's eyes—a creature who had once been a tall, lanky, human man—until Kit returned home from work the next morning, but the now-inhuman thing's arm shot out as if from a cannon, breaking the spell, and smashing through the six-foot tall window pane with no more effort than a man punching through paper.

Kartya did not think, not in any conscious, deliberate manner. She ran to the stairs on reflex, sprinting up them two at a time, her body knowing where it was taking her, seeing her destination in her mind as clearly as an earlier scene from *Evil Dead*. Though it defied logic, though an hour ago it had been impossible, she had to get to the revolver if she wanted to survive. As she flew down the hall for the bedroom, she had the wherewithal to dart her arm into the bathroom and flip the switch, the overhead fixture bright enough to allow a half-moon of light to spill into the hallway.

It took all of Kartya's willpower not to shut and lock the bedroom door behind her, but knowing how easily the thing had infiltrated the ground floor, it would behoove her to leave the door open and see it coming. She grabbed the gun from the nightstand and slid along the front wall of the bedroom. Molding her hands around the butt in what she hoped was a relaxed position ("Never choke your gun," the range attendant had told her, "that's a surefire way to hit everything but your target"), she crouched by the closet, the thinnest rectangle of hallway visible from her spot on the floor.

The sound of footsteps shuffle-dragging up the stairs after her was interrupted by a second downstairs window imploding, and then, horribly, a third. Kartya wanted to curse. She wanted to scream, or cry, or curl up in the fetal position. Instead, she pulled the hammer back, prayed for consistency, squinted one eye, and kept utterly silent.

The thing made it to the top of the stairs and turned the corner. The hallway was short and Kartya had a clear shot, but she held fire. The thing took a long, lumbering step, then another. It wore jeans and a plaid flannel shirt with the sleeves rolled up, and as it stepped into the crescent of light filtering from the bathroom, Kartya saw strange marks on its forearms. The thing moved forward again.

The first shot shocked Kartya in its loudness, and she realized she'd never experienced gunfire firsthand without protective ear muffs. She recovered quickly, concentrating on readying a second shot despite the knowledge that the thing hadn't been halted or even slowed in its pursuit. She'd hit it three inches below the chest, a mark devoid of any major organs. Kartya hoped this was the only reason why the creature was still on its feet, but she had a sneaking suspicion that there was something more sinister spurring the demon forward.

Kartya hit the creature again, in the shoulder, and again, clipping its neck, spurts of blood exploding from the torn flesh, and again, another shot to the stomach. Still, it stalked toward her. Kartya took a deep breath and held it, steadying her hands and her gaze, and aimed for its right kneecap. She hit it dead center. The thing's leg folded backward, threatening to topple the creature ass over teakettle, but it would not go down. Before it could right itself, she aimed for the left kneecap. Another direct hit, and when the thing's jeans tore and knee shattered, Kartya saw a substantial fragment of bone go catapulting through the air like a haphazardly-thrown Frisbee. Again, the creature stayed on its feet.

Kit had considered the possibility of a break-in serious enough to warrant planting the revolver by her bedside, but not serious enough to provide her with extra bullets. The thing swayed like a drunken sorority girl in too-high heels, but when it took another step—hesitant, but advancing all the same—Kartya knew she had to enact Plan B.

Before she could change her mind, she rushed the thing with calculated strides, coming to a stop as she reached the end of the damask-patterned runner. She bent before the creature, loath to take her eyes off it for even a moment, and took the corner of the rug up in her fingers. She knew she couldn't yank the runner hard enough to accomplish her end goal of toppling the creature over the bannister and initiating a freefall to the ground floor below, but she hoped to knock it off its feet enough to start that process. Luck was on her side; the creature had already begun to fall off balance, so that when she yanked the runner with a throaty grunt, its back was already pressed against the bannister, and the upward movement of the rug functioned to throw the creature's legs up and over its head in a graceless backflip over the railing.

It fell the distance of fourteen hardwood steps and crashed to the floor below. Flipping on the hall light, Kartya leaned over and peered down. The thing had already gotten up and was placing one splintered but still-operational leg onto the bottom step.

"You have got be kidding me," Kartya said, scuttling back from the edge and heading for the guest bedroom.

Kartya had only fired the shotgun on one prior occasion, and even then she'd almost passed on the opportunity, preferring to refine her technique with the handgun. Before she exited the bedroom, she slipped her still-bare feet into a pair of red Victoria's Secret slippers, the left foot embroidered with the word *naughty* in white stitching, and the right with the word *nice*. It occurred to her that it would be immeasurably easier to fight Deadites without a full bladder, so she walked to the bathroom to relieve herself, pointing the shotgun at an opening in the bannister rails as she did, counting herself lucky when she heard what sounded like a scuffle amongst the creatures at the bottom of the stairs, delaying their climb. She declined to flush, not sure if the noise would send their zombie-like brains into a frenzy, and stood at the threshold of the passage to the stairs. *What would Ash do?* she thought. She looked down at her feet.

"Time to put the naughty foot forward," she said, forcing a half-grin, and stepped her left foot out into the hallway.

Kartya thudded down the stairs, took in the scene below her, and cocked the shotgun. There were three creatures, as she'd guessed from the equal number of shattered windows, and they appeared more akin to Deadites than she'd have thought possible, seeing as she wasn't on-set for a taping of *Ash vs Evil Dead*. They were undeterred by pain but incapable of reason, and they were unable to begin their onslaught of the second floor because they couldn't decide amongst the three of them who was going to go up first. Kartya helped them out by blowing the arm off the shorter, stocky man on the left, who looked down to regard the blood and sinew hanging from his shoulder with puzzled detachment.

The thing to the right of the tall creature had been female in its human form. Kartya made the mistake of pulling the trigger as she moved down another step, throwing off her aim and catching the she-thing in the upper portion of the skull, blowing off the top half of its scalp, rocking the thing's head back on its neck. The head snapped back to its original position. Kartya recalled the catchphrase of the popular children's toy that refused to be bowled over: "Weebles wobble, but they don't fall down." With dark amusement, she wondered if anyone had tried to knock a Weeble down with a double-barrel shotgun.

Kartya told herself to focus on this next shot. She aimed for the center of the tall one's head. "Boom," she said, a second before she squeezed the trigger.

The shot was absolute in its devastation, the shell forging a hole in the thing's skull like the point of a pastry-bag digging through a jelly-filled donut. Kartya was ecstatic to see that with its brain dislodged and projected somewhere into her living room, the Deadite-thing was finally incapable of pursuit.

So that's it, she thought. *They don't appear human, but they can be killed as such.* The Necronomicon proposed three specific ways to release a possessed soul: a live burial, bodily dismemberment, or purification by fire. Thinking that she liked her house, and would rather not burn it to the ground, and that time did not permit the digging of two graves in frozen soil, Kartya re-cocked the shotgun. Wistfully, she pictured Ash's chainsaw hand. Bodily dismemberment would be a hell of a lot easier with her hero's weapon of choice than by the excruciatingly slow process of fortuitous shotgun hits, but beggars can't be choosers.

Oblivious to the flecks of blood and brain matter peppering her body, Kartya closed the distance between her and the two evil things still standing. Needing to make it to the front door, she had to descend the stairs low enough to shoot the creatures sideways, preferably one to the right and one to the left. Getting within arm's reach of the things was not her idea of a good time, but neither was wasting two barrels of the shotgun into anywhere but their heads.

Kartya had properly determined the direction the undead things would be propelled in, but she wasn't lucky enough to replicate the angle of her shot to the taller creature's head. Though the things were knocked to the floor and out of her path, they were reanimating quicker than she would have liked.

Imitating a move she'd seen one of Ash's badass sidekicks perform, Kartya barrel-rolled across the back of the couch, vaulted over the coffee table, and grabbed the plastic *Evil Dead* toys from their speakers. As she charged the Deadites, she pistoned one arm back, and released the action figure like a cannon. The *Army of Darkness* soldier's spear caught the first creature in the eye. Kartya lobbed mini Ash Williams, and it wedged between the second creature's rot-infested open maw.

"Yes!" Kartya cheered as she swiped her car keys from

their hook. Without looking back, she fled into the cold night in only her slippers, sweatpants, and an ash-grey t-shirt, darkened in several places with the demon-things' blood.

Ten steps down the front walkway and the moon made a glorious reappearance, lighting Kartya's path to the garage and keeping her from tripping on a bizarre pile of items laid out at the base of the driveway. Allowing a second for curious inspection, Kartya stooped and beheld the needles, spoons, and a Dunkin Donuts cup of what appeared to be coffee-tainted water. Then the water hissed, geysering up from the cup in an angry spout, and she reevaluated her first interpretation.

"Crazed junkies or the infected victims of a science experiment gone wrong," she said as she jogged for the garage. "Either way, no fucking thanks."

The garage door groaned in protest as Kartya flung it open. She unlocked the Jeep's doors with a terse beep, praying the noise was not enough to attract the Deadites. She surveyed the driveway and as much of the yard as was visible: nothing came for her. Hopping into the car, thinking she could be at the police station in less than five minutes, hoping this was quick enough to bring back reinforcements before the creatures could abandon her place for somewhere else, she threw the car into reverse and prepared to backup. The stout male thing and the lone female one took up the entirety of her rearview mirror.

"I don't think so," Kartya whispered, and flooded the gas. The things disappeared under the Jeep and Kartya flinched as she registered the sounds of splitting flesh and crunching bone. It sounded like someone had thrown a cantaloupe onto pavement from six stories up. Then, there was quiet.

Kartya sat in the driver's seat, feeling her skin slide over the leather under its coating of gore. She had time for one profound exhalation before a figure blotted out the moonlight streaming through the passenger's side window. As she regarded the reanimated corpse-woman with horror, the driver's door opened and Kartya was pulled from the Jeep by a pair of rough hands inserted beneath her armpits.

At the last second, before her legs had passed the frame of the vehicle, she found purchase and launched herself backward. The thing hit the pavement again with a wet thump, and Kartya managed to disentangle herself from its clutches.

She ran for the garage, hoping to find a pair of gardening shears. Instead, her headlights illuminated a beautiful sight, the most beautiful sight she'd ever seen. She said a silent apology for ever nagging Kit about cleaning out the garage, packed full with junk from previous tenants, and sprinted for the chainsaw.

She flipped the switch and placed the saw on the dusty floor, gripping the handlebar with her left hand.

"Here goes everything," she said, and pulled the recoil rope like she'd seen her father, Kit, and Ash all do on numerous occasions. The saw popped, but did not start.

"Dammit!" She watched the first of the possessed-things, which after its run-in with her Jeep had lost even a passing resemblance to a living human, approach the mouth of the garage. She jimmied a black lever on one side and tried the starter rope again. The saw came to life with a deafening rumble.

Kartya had been a vegetarian for eight years, so the extent of her experience with chopping flesh was limited. By the time she'd finished a violent vertical dismemberment of the stout man, she was so thoroughly covered in blood that she did not imagine the second creature's vivisection could be any worse. It was coming for her, the female, and though Kartya almost slipped in the lake of blood that covered the two-car garage from wall-to-wall, she was ready for it.

"You're taller than Chuckles over there, so this could take a while," Kartya told the demon-thing.

Kartya missed the creature's hellish reply under the unforgiving tremors of the chainsaw.

—

Headlights announced the approach of a vehicle. Drenched from head to foot with an unfathomable amount of blood, Kartya was not curious as to the identity of the driver until the car passed the entrance to No Bottom Pond Road and started down the driveway. Wiping a film of blood from around her eyes, she was surprised to see Kit's Volkswagen nearing the carnage.

When the car turned and illuminated the blood-covered specter that was Kartya, Kit threw the car in park and was at her side in seconds.

"What the hell! Where—?" His hands grasped her shoulders and he surveyed her wildly, looking for a wound.

"It's not my blood," Kartya told him. She gestured behind her where four halves equaled two bodies.

Kit's jaw dropped.

"I'll explain, but we should call the police. They took some sort of recreational drug that turned out to be far from recreational. It infected them with something that turned them into zombies. Or... Deadites." She said these last words as if, despite the very concrete evidence of chaos behind her, Kit would think she'd lost her mind at the mention of the purportedly fictional walking dead.

"I can't believe this. I'm so glad you're all right. I pulled into the lot at work and thought *what the hell am I doing?* The night after the holiday, the night our friends get robbed, I shouldn't have left you. I should have been here for you. So I called in sick and came home. You should have called me, Kartya. No, you should have called the police right away!"

Moved past the point of revulsion at Kartya's blood-saturated state, Kit pulled her into a savage embrace. She let him hug her, still a bit shell-shocked, then stepped back and took it all in.

The gore packed into her Jeep's tire treads winked in the moonlight. The dismembered bodies glistened in wide pools of blood near the still-purring chainsaw. The pile of syringes and infected water sat in the foreground of the house's smashed windows. The house itself, a looming skull with its two front teeth knocked out. Her eyes came back to settle on Kit, and she smiled.

"There was no time to call anyone. I didn't have much in the way of options, didn't have time to come up with a plan. I had to rely on myself, I guess. With a little inspiration from a certain groovy guy." She paused, wiped a smear of blood from her cheek, and continued, "The important thing is that I did what needed to be done, and that I'm okay. And you're home now... so come here, and gimme some sugar, baby."

A FAIRY PLANT IN GRIEF

Her boots crunched on the gritty snow and the sound reminded her of the hard candies she and her sister used to devour at the back of her parents' store. They would huddle together behind towering boxes of soft drinks (their favorites were the Clearly Canadians in the elegant glass bottles, as smooth and sensual as a lady's silhouette) and suspend the candies under one another's nose and guess which kind the other held.

There were few things in the grey-scale palette of the graveyard that recalled those colorful candies of her youth, but the longer she walked, the better her chances were of finding what she needed. It was a shame that the flowers she'd amassed could not retain their colors. In the ramshackle Victorian on Elm Street that had once been her parents', but now belonged to her and her sister, dried bouquets of flowers covered every available surface of wall, upside down and desiccated like a silent colony of bats.

Mikhail would occasionally grip the dried-out petal of one of these inverted flowers—the coagulated-blood maroon of a hybrid tea rose, the thin, claw-like spear of a dahlia—and rub her fingers so that the petal disintegrated like overburdened tissue paper, or the wings of an insect left to wither on a windowsill. She'd regret this once the act was done, did not like to squander the fruits of many laborious hunts, but sometimes she was unable to help her anger at this degradation of beauty, at the flowers that had made promises of comfort and distraction, but faded and shrunk and aged like everything else that was, and everything that would be.

Mikhail walked a meandering path through the cemetery, looking for a break from stone and marble on the cold December day. She'd made it as far as the river when she stumbled onto a private moment between a couple—hand-in-hand, their cheeks moist with tears—and a ghost. She had to wait and whistle, appear otherwise engaged until these harbingers of color ceased their whispered prayers and retreated through the thick iron gates, back to the land of the living.

The flowers were exquisite in the glaring winter sun and it hurt Mikhail's heart to look at them. She ran her fingers along liquid amber and chocolate cosmos, across the snow-white petals of sweet peas, and the waxy surfaces of dusty millers and viburnum blueberries. Then, after glancing around to ensure she was alone, save for the crows and the velvety-winged swallowtails, she snatched up the arrangement, folded it beneath her sweater, and started out toward home.

The house was sepulchral-quiet upon her return and she paused at the kitchen sink to spritz her prize with water. She kicked off the clunky boots before ascending the stairs, her socked feet noiseless on the polished wood. Light, the faintest of glowing embers, leaked into the hallway from under the bedroom door. She hesitated, pinching off the browned corner of a Sahara rose petal, and let it flutter to the floor. She pushed the door open and pasted a smile on her face, the action suffused with all the care of a florist preparing a bouquet.

"I'm back," she said to the motionless body on the bed. "I brought you something."

She plucked an arrangement of dying flowers from the nightstand and replaced it with the vibrant assemblage of peaches and corals, burgundies and scarlets. She took her sister's cold hand and looked upon the eyelids, purplish and closed and like twin buds that had been snipped too soon, never to open again.

"Guess," she said, holding the bouquet under her sister's nose. "Guess what kind of flowers I have brought for you today?"

WOLVES AT THE DOOR AND BEARS IN THE FOREST

Cheek pressed against a peeling linoleum floor, one arm bent at a painful angle behind her back, Molly Monteith set her gaze on a small plastic baggie, cloudy with the remnants of whatever narcotic it had recently held, and watched as it trembled in the weak pulse of the grease-stained radiator. If she'd been closer, she could have fished the baggie from under that radiator and ran it over her gums, mining the plastic for whatever relief it held.

Before she could grit her teeth against the pain, Klay Shoemaker flipped her onto her back and sent her skull into the side of the coffee table. She closed her eyes against the trickling blood and willed her muscles to go limp so that the bear of a man, breathing hard and sheened with sweat, could drag her onto a rug discolored by a decade of overturned beers.

I'm not here, Molly thought. *I'm floating far away from here... flying high above the pain.*

Molly's chewed-up fingernails clicked against the linoleum. Her landlord grinned wolfishly, squeezed her breasts, and backhanded her across the face. Molly winced and saw stars. She tasted blood, but she did not make a sound. She never let on to Klay that she was anything other than grateful for their arrangement. For the exchange of sex-for-rent that seemed to become more tyrannical and horrific the more Molly's situation warranted it.

When she finally limped from Klay's apartment, she had a receipt for the month of December. That had been her stipulation: he could do whatever he wanted to her as long as Molly was granted proof of payment.

Molly opened the door to the apartment below Klay's, recoiling at its identical layout, at the knowledge that flashbacks of her torments would visit her at inopportune moments.

Nothing destroys the illusion of normalcy like passing your abusive landlord on the way out to the park. She pulled the door shut and crept to the apartment's only bedroom, a room she'd painstakingly labored over until it was a chamber fit for a princess atop a tower.

Her stomach dropped at the sight of her daughter already awake, but her pulse steadied when she realized Audrey had yet to slip from between the covers. Audrey was captivated by the bedraggled Teddy Ruxpin reading her a story, unaware that her mother had only just returned.

As she watched her daughter grasp the bear's shabby paw, Molly's hand traveled up to the swollen ruin of her mouth. She let her mind wander to the contents of the cupboards and thought she'd suffer the same treatment from the grocer if it meant more food in Audrey's stomach. Her probing fingers dug too hard at her lip and she gasped. Audrey looked up.

"Mommy!" Audrey held her arms in an entreaty to be lifted from the bed.

Molly stepped forward and grimaced. "Climb out of bed like a big girl," she said, willing her pain to go unnoticed. "What would you like for breakfast?"

Audrey slid from the four-poster bed before dragging Teddy after her. "Pancakes!" she declared and skipped into the hallway, thumping the bear's heavy body against her mother's leg.

Molly stifled a cry. "Go find your juice cup," she managed. "And set the table. Mama will make you some pancakes." Audrey scampered away to comply.

"Audrey?" Molly called after her daughter.

"Yeah, Mommy?"

"I love you all the world."

"I love you too, Mommy."

"As much as anything in all the world?"

Audrey turned and smiled at her mother. "As much as all the world, Mommy." The girl paused, noticing Molly's injuries. "What's that boo-boo on your face?"

"It's nothing, sweetheart. Mommy walked right into the cabinet getting some water this morning. It's like in *One More Spot* when Teddy paints the black dots on the ladybug's shell, only I've got one on my face!"

Audrey's mouth scrunched as she tried to work out something too complex for her three short years, but the comparison of the bruise to something from a storybook, coupled with the prospect of pancakes, was enough to set the girl back on her path to the kitchen.

By the time Molly had cleaned herself up, Audrey was seated at the table, humming the intro to the Teddy Ruxpin tapes as she attempted to fold a paper towel into a seashell, a smile on her heart-shaped face.

Audrey never asked for anything, but she had begged her mother for the revamped smart model of the talking teddy Molly herself had adored as a kid. At a hundred bucks a pop, Molly couldn't afford a new bear, so she'd journeyed across town to her grandmother's old colonial where she spent the afternoon in an airless attic, sidestepping dead mice and searching through talismans of memories best left undisturbed.

When she'd found her old companion stuffed inside a box with the complete collection of cassette tapes, she'd worried Audrey would prefer no bear at all to the poor excuse for the technologically advanced one the other kids boasted. But here Audrey sat in mute fascination as the plastic, cartoon mouth opened and closed in time to the words of the story.

The dented box of Bisquick was the only thing in the cupboard besides a jar of pickles and a can of tomato soup. Audrey hated all things tomato, but soup—specifically, tomato soup—was a staple at the local food pantries. Weeks would elapse where nothing but the thick paste of the condensed Campbell's Classic passed Molly's lips, so intent was she on saving the chicken noodle and occasional can of hearty chili for her daughter.

Molly went to work on the pancakes, and had served Audrey the first batch when the girl said, "Mommy, do we not have to go to the clinic today?"

Molly dropped the spatula and shot a look at the stovetop clock. It was blinking. She rushed to the couch and rifled through her purse, ignoring a photo of Audrey at the pumpkin patch the previous month to stare in rising panic at the time on her phone.

"Fuck!" she shouted and threw her purse over one shoulder. She flew to the table and gripped Audrey's arm, lifting her from the chair and dragging her toward the door.

"But my pancakes! I didn't eat my pancakes yet!"

"You can eat them when we get back! We have to go now!"

Molly held the keys to the twenty-year old Civic between shaking fingers and closed her eyes.

"Start, you bitch," she whispered.

The engine sputtered, caught, and died.

"No!" The word burst from her mouth like geese exploding off the bank of a lake. Audrey whimpered from the backseat. Molly pulled the keys from the ignition and held them, poised for a miracle. "Please just fucking start," she begged.

Molly let forth with an astonished laugh when the engine caught and held. She'd made the first few lights on a busier-than-usual Main Street and was beginning to relax when a line of brake lights roused her from her reverie. She slammed her foot in time to avoid rear-ending the Mercedes in front of her, and then sat in a horrified, incredulous silence for the twelve minutes it took for the crew to pull the fallen spruce from the road.

It was exactly eleven AM when Molly pulled into the lot for the Somersworth branch of the clinic, her stomach knotted with anxiety, her heart lodged high in her throat.

"Wait here," she croaked, and shut the door before Audrey could protest. She sprinted up the cement walkway. The women passing her in the opposite direction gave her pitying looks.

The towering figure of Victoria Swanson stood at the intersection of lobby and hallway, blocking Molly's view of the dosing windows and increasing the flow of adrenaline to Molly's veins. The Program Director's face was as calm and imperial as ever beneath a grey spiked bob.

"Dosing is closed," Victoria said. Steve, the Clinical Director, stood beside her.

"Please," Molly whispered, looking back and forth between them. "It's eleven now."

She spun to where the nurses still bustled behind their respective windows, cleaning the pumps, entering their notes. Molly caught Melissa's eye. Melissa was around Molly's age, with a daughter of her own. The nurse looked quickly away.

"I haven't been on the clinic long," she tried, frantic, ignoring the callousness in their eyes. "If I don't get my dose, I'll be sick. Please. I don't want to be sick all night."

"This is not a discussion, Ms. Monteith," Victoria said, her words devoid of emotion. "New Hampshire state law prohibits the distribution of methadone from the computerized pumps after eleven AM."

Victoria turned to Steve and asked him something Molly did not hear. He responded with the name of the counselor Molly saw for one-to-one sessions.

Victoria gestured toward the secretary at the front desk. "Would you like Cindy to see if Olive is available? Perhaps talking to your counselor would be beneficial."

Molly wanted to scream that talking to her counselor wouldn't do shit. She wanted to rail against the state laws that mandated the dosing hours of a privately owned clinic. But more than that, she wanted to inflict pain onto herself. She hated herself for losing track of time while she was fucking her landlord, hated herself for getting on methadone when she'd left detox. Most of all, she hated herself for being a heroin addict in the first place.

Molly felt Victoria and Steve looking at her, taking in her swollen lip and disheveled hair. She colored when she realized she had slippers on her feet.

"I can't see my counselor right now," Molly repeated. "I have Audrey in the car."

Molly watched as Victoria's expression morphed into one of actual emotion, then blanched as she realized that emotion was alarm.

"Ms. Monteith," the Program Director began, "are you

aware that the temperatures have been close to freezing for much of the past week?"

Molly did not answer. *I'm floating*, she thought. *Floating above this nightmare.*

"And are you aware that as mandated reporters, the staff at this clinic is required to alert the Department of Children and Families of any instances of child abuse or neglect?"

Molly still said nothing. *I'm flying. Far away from this clinic, and this life.*

"Leaving a child alone in a freezing car isn't a sound show of judgement, Ms. Monteith."

Molly's panic was all-consuming. "No! I left her with..." Who was the woman she'd passed on the way in? She'd attended group counseling with her for a few weeks after being admitted to the clinic and had chatted with the woman more than once. "Jordan!" she said triumphantly, as Victoria had opened her mouth to speak. "Jordan was keeping an eye on her while I ran inside. I passed her on my way in."

Molly darted for the exit, her heart jackhammering in her chest. "I'll make sure I'm on time tomorrow," she said. It now seemed far more important to get out of there without Victoria reporting her to DCF than it did to get her dose. Molly opened the door and sprinted outside.

What had she been thinking? It was freezing, so how could she have left Audrey in the car?

She was so shaken from the confrontation inside the clinic that it didn't occur to her to be thankful the Civic started on the first try. She sped from the parking lot, turning onto Route 108.

"Mm—mommy," Audrey said from the backseat, "I'm re—really, really hungry." The girl was shivering, and her cheeks were wet; she'd been crying while Molly had been gone.

"Right," Molly said. A pack of cigarettes was tucked into the crease of the passenger seat, and Molly threw it to the floor when she discovered it was empty. She squinted at the Dunkin Donuts ahead. It would be a splurge, but she could bum a cigarette and appease Audrey at the same time. "How about some Munchkins?" Molly sing-songed. "If we go to Dunks, will you forgive me for pulling you away from your pancakes this morning?

She'd meant it as a joke, but Audrey considered this question solemnly. Molly's chest tightened above bruised ribs.

"I gu—guess," the little girl said.

The Dunkin Donuts off Route 108 was an extension of the clinic parking lot—the stage on which many a drama went down—and Molly remembered this upon observing the countless cars and the sea of familiar faces through the plate-glass windows. She tried to convince Audrey that the drive-thru would be just as fun, but Audrey wouldn't hear it and Molly owed her at least this one small indulgence.

Coffee and greasy bags of donuts in hand, Molly scanned the restaurant for a place to sit. She was about to tell Audrey that it looked like they were going to have to eat in the car after all when Molly's assumed babysitter, Jordan, gestured to Molly. Molly hesitated, then wondered if she could let Jordan in on the white lie she'd told Victoria. She ushered Audrey forward.

Jordan made room for Audrey, while Jordan's friend pulled a chair over for Molly.

"Thanks," Molly said, burning her tongue on her coffee. "It's been one of those days."

"Yeah?" Jordan studied Molly. "We were wondering about that. You miss your dose?"

Molly blinked, embarrassed to find that tears stung her eyes.

"What are you going to do?" Jordan's friend asked. "Sorry," she blushed. "I'm Cassie. I don't mean to be nosy, it's just that I missed my dose last week for the first time. I know how you feel."

"What can I do?" Molly said. "I've got to grin and bear it 'til tomorrow."

Jordan and Cassie exchanged a look, and panic rose in Molly's chest, a feeling that was becoming as common as a wellspring that rose with the rain. Did they doubt her intention to stay clean? The last thing Molly needed was a second instance of her ability to mother Audrey called into question in a single morning. Jordan dipped a chunk of muffin into her latte. Cassie fished a lip gloss out of her sweatpants pocket and applied a fresh coat.

"It totally sucks though," Jordan said a moment later. "Being sick. It's like when you're first getting stable on the clinic and they take for-goddamn-ever to bring you up on your dose. They make you fill out a form with your counselor once you've been coming a certain number of days, so every time you want to go up, it's like an act of Congress."

"Did you hear about when Kristy Hughes first got admitted?" Cassie asked.

"Of course," Jordan said. "Who hasn't?"

They looked at Molly and saw that Molly hadn't.

"Tell, tell," Jordan goaded Cassie, "Molly wants to know."

"Well, Kristy was on Valium, had, like, PTSD from an abusive relationship, but they told her she was on too high of a dose and made her taper off. At the same time, her counselor followed the clinic's smoking cessation policy and recommended Kristy get on Chantix. They brought her up on her dose at a snail's pace and she was constantly complaining of withdrawals. Between that, being off her Valium, and the severe depression that came with the Chantix, Kristy—"

"She tried to kill herself," Jordan interjected.

Molly took a long swallow of coffee and tried to recall if she'd ever been in group with a Kristy Hughes. The name didn't ring a bell, but it was harder to concentrate and she had a general sense of unease that had nothing to do with her current company. It also seemed unfathomable to have been craving a cigarette.

Don't tell me I'm going into withdrawal already.

Cassie and Jordan were still talking, debating the plausibility of another recent rumor they'd heard through the clinic grapevine. Molly rubbed her temple and tried to focus.

"Johnny P. said he saw it with his own eyes!" Cassie was saying.

"Johnny P. is full of shit!" Jordan said, matter-of-fact. "He also never leaves his mother's basement, so I'm not buying a story that involves him hiking through the Scoutland trails any more than I believe him when he says it was the lab's fault his drug screens were dirty."

Molly smiled weakly. "Sorry, I zoned out for a second. What about hiking in the woods?"

Cassie turned to Molly. "You know the woods in Rollinsford? Well, those trails are a popular place for people looking to get high. There've been... reports from those who've gone into the forest, claiming that one second, they're alone with their drugs, and the next, they look up to see a set of stairs in the woods."

"They're not, like, part of a demolished stone wall or anything like that," Jordan clarified. "They're stairs right out of Suburbia, USA, only smack in the middle of the woods!"

"Stairs?" Molly echoed, confused. "Why would there be stairs in the woods?"

"No one knows," Cassie said. "But everyone who's seen them describes them the same."

"If you go looking for them," Jordan said, in a tone appropriate for telling ghost stories around a campfire. "If you go to the exact same spot where they were last seen... they're gone!"

"Have you looked for them yourself?" Molly asked.

"Well, no," Jordan admitted, "but Cassie's friend, Crystal, she's friends with Nicole Price, and Nicole's boyfriend, Eddie, and he says that he was walking one of his dogs in the woods and threw a stick way ahead of them on the trail. When he caught up to the dog, it was standing there at the edge of a clearing, looking up at a set of stairs."

"Did he get a picture?" Molly asked.

"No," Jordan said, disappointed. "I guess he didn't have his phone with him."

Molly yawned. Her eyes watered, and her nose ran. Cassie studied her knowingly.

Molly feigned ignorance. "I've had a bit of a cold lately. It's been freezing all week and my landlord's a dick. We're lucky if the thermostat sees sixty all winter."

"Right," Cassie said. She glanced at Audrey, who was still distracted by her talking teddy bear. "So what do you think? Will you make it until tomorrow without calling your old dealer?"

Cassie's eagerness broke through the fog of Molly's methadone-starved brain. She realized how stupid she'd been to share anything with these women. Even the most mundane details of her life were fodder for the gossip mill, and now Cassie and Jordan knew that she was in dire straits until tomorrow morning. She shuddered as she thought of how close she'd come to letting Jordan in on the lie she'd told Victoria. Better to keep quiet and hope for the best.

Molly almost toppled her chair as she stood. "I have to go. Thanks for sharing the table."

Molly looked back at the two women before she and Audrey slipped from the restaurant. Leaning over the table, heads almost touching, they were too engaged in conversation to notice.

It was eight by the time she'd put Teddy aside to read Audrey a bedtime story of her own. She'd quelled the shaking of her fingers in order to smooth the girl's hair, and set her teeth against the ache of her muscles as she pulled the covers tight across Audrey's tiny frame.

The sun had retreated from the sky, pulling its patterns of light from the walls and floor with it as it went, leaving a world of shadow in its wake. Molly stood in the living room like the survivor of a shipwreck, unsure how to get through a night that stretched before her like the sea.

The voices told her to abandon her resolve, to throw it all away while her daughter slept, to look at the squalor of her life, at the bruises on her body and the layers of scar tissue that marred the crooks of her arms, and pose the obvious question: what was the point?

She walked to the bathroom compelled by the apocalyptic feeling that accompanied every stage of opioid withdrawal. She rummaged through the medicine cabinet until she'd amassed a decent stash: Trazadone, Nyquil, the Gabapentin Audrey's father had given her years before, and a Clonidine script that bore the name of her old roommate.

Alone, none of the medications would go far toward alleviating her distress. If she was lucky, the Trazadone and Nyquil would help her sleep, the Gabapentin would assuage her restless legs, and the Clonidine would lower her blood pressure enough to keep her calm. Molly knew the clinic would consider this instance of self-medication a relapse, but if she could get through the night without reaching for her phone, she'd call it a success.

Molly laid everything out on the coffee table and lowered herself onto the couch. She would try to sleep while she still could and take the medication—like a Band-Aid on a bullet wound—when the withdrawals were unendurable.

—

Molly did not immediately recognize the thunderous banging as someone knocking on the door. When she sprang from the couch, nausea and anxiety hit her like a tsunami. She crossed the apartment in three long strides, and before she could speculate who was on the other side, Molly gripped the frame and flung the door open.

The woman was younger than Molly, but in her smart navy suit and pearls, clipboard under one arm, she seized the upper hand straightaway. Her blond hair was pulled back into a low, tight bun, and her cardigan enveloped a body sculpted by Pilates.

The man was close in age to the clipboard-wielding woman, caramel-skinned, bespectacled, and apologetic. Molly realized what was happening too late; her reaction to the Division of Children, Youth, and Families on her doorstep only made things worse. She kicked at the door, trying to shut it in the woman's face, but the woman caught it and pushed it open again, Molly's sluggish limbs no match for reflexes unimpaired by withdrawal.

"Ms. Monteith? I'm Kate Shephard and this is my colleague, Henry Mendoza. We received a report on the possible neglect of a child under your care. May we come in?"

Kate Shephard did not wait for a reply. She walked past Molly and into the apartment, her head on an immediate swivel. "Where is your daughter now?" she asked.

"She's sleeping," Molly said. "You can look in her room if you want. I'm sorry I tried to shut the door on you, I didn't mean to, I panicked and..."

Kate was surveying the mess of dirty pans on the stove, the mixing bowl caked with batter, the juice glasses attracting fruit flies.

"I... I was late this morning and didn't have time to clean up."

"Late for the clinic, is that right?' Kate asked. She glanced at her notes. "But you missed your dose regardless, if I understand correctly. That's when you left your three-year-old daughter alone in the car to plead your case despite the knowledge that the clinic is bound by law from administering methadone after eleven AM?"

Molly's stomach churned with fear and rage. "It was only for a second," she stammered. She turned to look at the closed door of Audrey's room. If she could only get them to peek in on Audrey, in the room that was right out of a fairy tale, at the clean, warm comforter Audrey slept under, and the posters and books and toys and clothes that lined the walls and shelves, then everything would be okay. But Kate had no interest in observing Audrey; Kate only wanted to judge Molly and all her failings as a mother.

"And she wasn't alone. I had asked a friend to watch her."

"Right. A Jordan Pendelson," Kate said, referring to her notes again. "We spoke to Ms. Pendelson, Ms. Monteith. She said you never approached her with a request to look after your daughter. She also said that you were not feeling well when she saw you at Dunkin Donuts this morning and that she doubted your ability to care for your daughter in the face of withdrawal."

Molly felt as if her organs had been replaced with stones.

Kate continued, "We will be opening an investigation into your parenting of Audrey Monteith. Please be present at our Somersworth office on Monday at nine AM, with Audrey in tow, at which time we will begin the proceedings to determine if your daughter should remain in the home with you or be removed from your care. If you fail to—"

Kate's voice ceased to have form or meaning as Molly's gaze travelled to the coffee table. There, her insurance policy against withdrawal was splayed out for anyone to see, the dayglow orange of the prescription bottles in stark contrast to the table's light wood. She said a quick prayer, desperate for Kate to remain unaware of the cache, for Henry's eyes to refrain from alighting on the names on the prescription bottles, the names that were not her own.

Molly flashed back to the scene, twenty-five years earlier, when she'd been ripped from her own mother's bruised and bleeding arms and placed in the back of a social services van. She couldn't let that happen to Audrey. Molly maneuvered herself between the state workers and the pile of drugs on the coffee table, and when Kate's monologue came to an end, Molly responded without hesitation.

"I understand," she said.

For a beat after her reply, Molly felt the universe shrink to the few square feet separating Kate Shephard from Molly's potential ruin, and Kate seemed to intuit Molly's simmering terror. She suppressed an exhalation of relief when Kate turned to Henry, made a final admonishment for Molly not to be late on Monday, and nodded for him to follow her out of the apartment.

With that, Molly was alone. Understanding seemed divorced from thought, and she stood, unmoored, in the center of the room. Her breathing came in ragged gasps, her body unable to withstand the torment of withdrawal when coupled with the mental agony of the ramifications of the state workers' visit. She spun toward the coffee table, planning to jump the gun on the pharmaceutical grab bag of relief. She stopped mid-stride.

In the tapestry of her mind, a seam ripped opened. Through that hole, a tempest blew.

Molly sprinted out the door and up the stairs before she could talk herself out of what she was about to do. It occurred to her, as she banged on Klay Shoemaker's door, that there were a million things wrong with her plan. Klay might be out, or have company, another woman he billed with his fists and his fury, another woman who breathed in mouthfuls of his filthy, beer-smelling rug while pieces of her soul cracked off and drifted away, never to be recovered.

Following the creak of hinges, Klay's massive form filled the doorframe. He was backlit by the glow of a television, beer in hand. A pungent wave of sweat and marijuana seeped into the hall.

"I need a favor," Molly said. She felt both piercing shame and monstrous anticipation. Flip sides of the same daedalian coin.

Klay leered knowingly. "You here to pay January in advance?"

Molly grimaced but forced herself to press on.

"Something important has come up and I have to run out. I should be back in a half hour, forty-five minutes, tops. Do you think you could watch TV in my apartment until then and keep an eye on Audrey for me?"

Klay couldn't keep the surprise from his face.

"What the hell, Molly? I ain't no babysitter. What do you have to go do?" His eyes narrowed. "You ain't going to do what I think you're going to do, are you?"

"Of course not! But I can't get into it right now. Can you do this for me? Please? I've got a fifty-inch flat screen," she said.

She refrained from telling him she hadn't had cable in months.

Klay sighed. "I guess. Jesus. You're going to owe me for this. Know what I mean?"

"I know. Whatever you say."

Molly's mind was already five steps ahead. It was with monumental effort that she came back to the present.

"Audrey's sleeping and should stay that way until I get back. If she happens to wake up, give her a glass of milk, stick a tape in her Teddy Ruxpin, and tell her I'll be home before it gets to the end of the story. Got it?"

—

No matter how long Molly stayed clean, her dealer's phone number never changed. With the heroin in her pocket, the world Molly traversed that night was a different one. The moon was full, but the sky was starless, and Molly walked in search of the perfect place, the Civic having finally shit the bed. The last cruel affront in a day—no, a lifetime—full of them.

The town was strung with Christmas lights, but their splendor fell far short of penetrating Molly's consciousness.

Molly walked until she no longer felt the cold through her slippers. She walked until the swishing of her arms against her threadbare jacket lulled her into numbness. She walked until the lights of the town fell away and the moon was as bright as the sun. She walked until the buildings and shops gave way to long stretches between houses, then to farmland, then to woods.

When she'd walked long enough for there to be nothing around her but miles of forest and the yellow, uncaring eyes of nocturnal things, she stopped.

She set up quickly against the trunk of a great tree, the muscle memory required for the pouring, mixing, and drawing up almost as ingrained as the muscle memory of stroking her daughter's face after she'd woken from a nightmare. The euphoria that flooded her brain and body was like slipping into a hot spring after being cold for an eternity, and she let herself go with it, let herself be carried away on a wave that would not crash.

When she opened her eyes, the edges of the forest, the angles of its trees, its peaks and valleys, seemed softer and less pronounced, its mist-draped colors more muted. A gleaming cherry wood staircase sat in the middle of a clearing. The moon cast a spotlight on the first step.

Molly stared at the staircase, a sense of loss befalling her, but also one of peace. It was the sense that if she made the decision to walk up those stairs, things would be better. Better for her, but more importantly, better for Audrey.

Molly realized the decision had already been made.

She rose, her slippers shuffling across the dampened leaves of the forest floor and walked toward the impossibility before her. She stopped at its base, considered the stairs' height and width, saw each step as a move away from all the unfortunate choices she'd made in her life, those best-laid-plans that had devolved into years of sorrow she could not shake.

She climbed.

The higher she ascended, the more she felt the forest forgive her for all her shortcomings. Her fear deserted her, then self-hatred.

On the last step, before Molly Monteith disappeared in the

quiet mist like a ship too far from shore, the very breath in her lungs dissolved into smoke, leaving her weightless and feeling like she could float... or fly.

THIS OUR ANGRY TRAIN

"On this train," the conductor says, "it doesn't matter if you have a ticket or not."

"On this train," Lauren counters, "a tired traveler just wants to show her ticket like anyone else."

If the Amtrak conductor is nonplussed by her dismissal, he doesn't show it. Lauren is worn-out and in no mood for flirtation. The conductor leans over and scans her e-ticket. The bright beam of alien light flashes red in her eyes before winking out.

Lauren places her hand on a hardcover suspense novel and looks at the conductor as if to ask *will that be all?* The conductor tips the shiny black brim of his hat to her, but makes no move to go.

The train's whistle is a long, mournful wail. Most of the curtains are drawn over the windows but Lauren's is open, giving her a view of the Back Bay station sign hanging in a tunnel made dreary by an excess of urine-stained concrete, scurrying rats, and abandoned newspapers flying like so many restless ghosts. The station sign swings, though there is no wind.

"This train is haunted," the conductor says.

"Haunted?" Lauren says. She's annoyed at the conductor's persistence, but she's intrigued as well.

"Yes, haunted. It is a vessel for lost souls moving from one place to the next. A vessel of memories."

Lauren sinks back against her seat. "That's not haunted," she says, with a wave of her hand. "That's just a train."

He leans in and begins to whisper:

> Against the kind and awful reign
> Of darkness, this our angry train,
> A noisy little rebel, pouts
> Its brief defiance, flames and shouts.

Lauren cocks her head at the mustached, rhyming conductor.

"It *is* haunted," he says. "They call this train, *The End of the Line*. The man that operates this train, this route, has done so for as long as anyone can remember. They say his wife and daughter were riding *The End of the Line* one dark and stormy night when the wheels hit a dislodged track at seventy miles per hour. The derailment caused the lead locomotive to crash into the side of a cliff bordering the tracks and explode. The impact caused a fuel spill, sparking a massive fire, while several other cars ended up in a nearby millpond. Forty-eight people lost their lives and one-hundred others were injured. The engineer's wife and daughter were killed instantly.

Lauren grimaces, but the conductor seems not to notice.

"Dozens of passengers saw him in the engineer car before the crash, but somehow, in the aftermath, he arrived at the site dressed not in his uniform but in street clothes, off duty. The engineer they pulled from the wreckage? His body was never identified.

"*The End of the Line* underwent major repairs, with most of the cars having to be completely replaced. And poor Erikson Cruz Shapiro had to bury empty coffins, his wife and daughter's bodies were so pulverized in the crash."

"Why are you telling me this?"

"Because no one else has," the conductor replies. "And because I always work with Shapiro. He likes having me on his train. Insists on it. I'm Mr. Holland by the way."

Mr. Holland extends one thin, gloved hand and Lauren shakes it. Holland returns his hand to his pocket.

"Shapiro's name was recorded in the log as the engineer the night of the crash, but he swore another operator requested a switch at the last minute. I testified to Shapiro's character after the crash. To his character and to his work ethic. All the passengers who claim to have seen Shapiro in the lead car the night of the accident said he was leering like a madman from his place behind the controls.

"The eyewitness reports were deemed unreliable, what with the traumatic nature of the crash and the phenomenon of false memories and all. With no other evidence, it was determined that Shapiro wasn't operating the train when it veered off course. The unidentified engineer could have been a passenger on the train that night, having hijacked the train from the real engineer."

Lauren notices how pale the conductor's skin is above his bushy mustache. Holland's eyes burn scarlet, scaring Lauren silly before she realizes his eyes are reflecting the red light of the ticket scanner he's begun fiddling with. "It is an interesting story," she says.

The conductor stares down the train car, lost in thought. Finally, he says, "Yes, Old Shapiro is something else. I'll let you get back to your book. But be careful. Trains are not the safest of places, and this one is particularly dangerous."

The conductor spins on a heel of polished leather and strolls away before Lauren can ask him what he means. Before she can ask him if he's still trying to scare her with ghost stories or if there's something else about *The End of the Line* she should know. She watches him walk the length of the car and disappear. There are no other passengers for whom he needs to check tickets. There are no other passengers at all.

Lauren resumes her reading, the thousand-page novel heavy in her lap, her eyelids heavier. She blinks emerald-amber eyes and gazes languidly out the window. The train is coming to a stop. Something catches Lauren's attention, a woman in black walking alongside the tracks. She says something to Lauren, unheard through the thick pane of glass and over the roar of a passing train. When all that's left of the eastbound train is a swirl of slowly settling dust, the woman is no longer a woman but a bird, a black sparrow flapping and cawing at Lauren in anger. Or in warning.

Its squabbling reaches Lauren's ears in the relative quiet of the train so recently departed:

He had a wife and a daughter and everyone said how lovely they were. His wife wanted to travel by train to visit her parents in Newport News but he forbade it. The woman booked a trip on The End of the Line *without telling him, believing she would be safe as long as he was behind the controls of the locomotive. He found her tickets and burned them in the hearth, placed a curse on her for her insubordination. Rebuffing the curse, the woman continued with her preparations, planning to repurchase her tickets at the gate. When she and her daughter left for the station, he was sitting in a tattered old armchair, staring at his grandfather's pocket watch. He refused to look at her despite the woman's attempts at reconciliation. She bid him farewell to no avail.*

When she arrived at the station, the woman was dismayed to find it overrun with sparrows. The fattest, blackest sparrows she had ever seen, hundreds of them, thousands even. There was talk of a delay; how would the engineer see through the flocks that had congregated on the tracks? Finally, the sparrows parted enough so that the train was able to move, and the woman and her daughter were on their way. The train derailed not long after it had reached full speed. The sparrows watched the rising smoke from the surrounding treetops. I should know, for I was one of the birds that witnessed these unfortunate events.

Lauren jerks awake at the completion of the sparrow's monologue. The car is cold and she reaches reflexively for her cell phone. She knocks it and it slips into the crack between the seats. Lauren thrusts her hand in after it. The air that accosts her groping fingers is frigid. It's as if she's plunged her hand into an icebox. Startled, Lauren pulls back, rubs her near-frozen fingers with the still-warm ones. The turquoise ring on the hand she pulled from between the seats drips with condensation.

Her phone is next to her on the seat. Lauren thinks that perhaps she has not fully wakened from her dream after all. Lauren thinks Mr. Holland might be right, that the train is haunted. Or at least, that its name, *The End of the Line*, fits it quite well.

None of the seats in her row will recline; the lights above her seat don't work; the electrical outlet won't charge her phone. She swears she put a bag of pretzels in the pocket of the seat in front of her, but when she reaches between Amtrak's on-board magazine and a forgotten issue of *Vogue*, there's nothing there. Lauren wonders if the car Shapiro's wife and daughter had died on was rundown like this one. She wonders if Holland remembers their names.

As if summoned by her thoughts, Holland appears in the aisle beside her. The muted light of the car gives him an ethereal quality. Holland looks as if he used to be a drinker, but has since given up the habit. He says:

> *Upon my crimson cushioned seat,*
> *In manufactured light and heat,*
> *I feel unnatural and mean.*
> *Outside the towns are cool and clean.*

Lauren gives him a curious look.

"Joyce Kilmer," he says. "American writer and poet known for a little ditty entitled, *Trees*. I prefer the one called *The Twelve Forty-Five*. I always have it stuck in my head. How's the ride treating you? Have you seen anything?"

"Seen anything?" Lauren echoes. "Like what?"

"Like ghosts. Rumor has it that Shapiro's wife and

daughter walk the tracks, trying to secure passage on *The End of the Line*. Sometimes they manage to hitch a ride, but it's never the right train. Travelers have seen them in the window of the quiet car. Screaming silent screams."

Lauren refrains from pointing out that people love to pass along urban legends, no matter how meager the kernel of truth from which they'd sprung.

Holland continues, "Their luggage makes its way onto *The End of the Line* every now and again. I've found it before, always after the last stop. No more passengers, yet two bags of luggage, one small and one large. As fast as I can, I go running for Shapiro, but by the time he gets to the back of the train, the bags have disappeared. It's gotten to where he no longer wants to be told of the bags' appearances. I think it's getting to him though." Holland's face is waxy and grey.

"What do you mean? Getting to him how?" Lauren asks.

"Shapiro's physical health isn't what it used to be. His mind even less so. A few weeks ago, I'm up in the lead car with him, letting him know we're all clear. *Do you see them, Holland?* he asks me. *Do you see the birds?* I look out ahead of us but all I see is an empty field. And the tracks. I told him, *No, sir. I don't see anything. They're there,* he says. *They're watching me. She's watching me.* I brought him a cup o' tea from the service car and he seemed better. Good enough to navigate at least. I'm worried about him, but what can I do?

"He's starting to follow his own schedule, too. Getting the train to where it's supposed to be on *his* time. Sometimes, not getting the train to where it's supposed to be at all. Just, sort of, rerouting it."

"Can he do that?"

"Sure he can do that. The average person would be amazed at how many directions these tracks run in. Last week, we were supposed to be in New York City, but we ended up in Albany. The passengers were mad as hell, but management won't do anything. To be honest, ever since the crash, they're afraid of him. Sure, it was determined Shapiro wasn't involved, but that doesn't mean people don't give him a wide berth. Shapiro has always been obstinate. He likes to go as the sparrow flies, as it were."

Lauren's blood freezes in her veins. "Did you say, as the sparrow flies?"

"Hmm? Oh. Yes, that's what I said." Holland walks back up the car, continuing his recitation of *The Twelve Forty-Five*:

> *The engine's shriek, the headlight's glare,*
> *Pollute the still nocturnal air*
> *The cottages of Lake View sigh*
> *And sleeping, frown as we pass by.*

Holland's footsteps die away. Lauren's thoughts wander. The reason Lauren is on the train is that she has met someone. A nice boy, as her mother would put it. She travelled to Boston in order to accept a dinner invitation, to eat spaghetti in the North End and look at the stars out over the wharf. Lauren wouldn't stay the night (she was, after all, a nice girl) and so she is on her way back to Mysticism, the small town between South Kingston and Westerly, Rhode Island she's lived in for seven years now.

Lauren tries to read to pass the time. She wears a monogramed pendant necklace and a layered sandstone maxi dress with wrap-up espadrilles, and her legs are cold. She folds her legs up under her and closes her eyes, her book tented over one knee.

It is even darker now, and the train screams though an ever blacker forest. Branches scrape along the windows like fingers too slow to drag their mummified bodies up from shallow graves. The moon twinkles like the lidless eye of some slippery beast.

The woman neither asks if the seat next to Lauren is taken, nor does she announce her presence in any other way. She sits next to Lauren as if they were old friends and Lauren's eyes snap open at the rustling beside her. A young girl, little more than a child, sits across the aisle and Lauren thinks she is with the woman, but she cannot be sure.

The woman smooths her black taffeta skirts and arches one sharply angled eyebrow. "Well," she says, "where are you coming from? Or, better yet, where are you going?"

"Mysticism," Lauren replies. Though she's miffed by all the impromptu conversation tonight, Lauren wasn't raised to be impolite, to ignore questions directed her way.

Perhaps her wariness shows on her face because the woman says, "You don't like the train, do you? Why do you fear it so?"

Lauren surprises herself by answering honestly. "Something terrible happened to me on a train once."

The woman nods, as if she understands this. "Me too," she says to Lauren.

The expression on Lauren's face mirrors the sadness etched in the lines of the woman's. Lauren tries to remain grounded in the present, but the veil shrouding the past slips away. A butterfly retiring into a cocoon and emerging as a caterpillar.

There was another train. In another time. His words come back to her, a warning to remain awake no matter what. There are dogs to stay away from, to keep from smelling her and what she carries, and she must not forget which station is her stop. Her skin—skin that was so hot in the heat of the outdoors—sprouts gooseflesh and she thinks, *If I'm quick, I can get away with it one more time.* The cloying scent of ammonia rushes into flared nostrils, the steel trap walls close her in, the taste of the poison slips down her scratchy throat. It was accidental. She's always maintained that it was accidental, now, and seven years ago after being removed from the train by police and EMTs.

The woman issues forth a light cough, interrupting Lauren's reverie. She regards Lauren with a calculating look, as if judging how much of Lauren's consciousness has returned to the here-and-now. Then, she says:

For what tremendous errand's sake
Are we so blatantly awake?
What precious secret is our freight?
What king must be abroad so late?
Perhaps Death roams the hills to-night
And we rush forth to give him fight.
Or else, perhaps, we speed his way
To some remote unthinking prey.

While the woman speaks, the little girl takes to twirling in the aisle, her cotton dress billowing out around scabbed knees.

"There are some things trains are good for," the woman says. "Like moving backward when you think you are moving forward." She looks past Lauren to the rushing world out the window. "Like now."

Lauren turns to look out the window of the train and experiences that sense of moving while sitting still. Or was it the opposite effect? Has Lauren been tricked into thinking they'd come to a stop while the train was moving? They could be traveling at one or one-hundred miles per hour and she wouldn't know the difference. If she were to step off the platform, would she plunge to her death, thrown like a ragdoll to become a human nest of skin and hair and broken bones? Would sparrows lay eggs in her mangled remains? Confused, Lauren turns back to her companion, but she—and the little girl—are gone.

When Lauren sits, motionless, and stares out the window at the passing landscape, she sees herself. First, it's merely her reflection. But then it morphs, a portal to the past. She sees the last few years of her life, the years since everything has been good. Years she worked hard for. A vision of well-paying jobs and men-to-take-home-to-mom and sophisticated friends and similar, safe endeavors.

The train hurtles through the darkness and Lauren sees the years before the good, when things were somewhere in-between good and bad. She sees the if-at-first-you-don't-succeed jobs, the scuffed waitress shoes, the late nights, the constant struggle to climb back to the low limb she'd clung to before the devastating fall. The in-between part—in its uncertainty and potential for capriciousness—might very well have been worse than the bad.

She thinks this only until she revisits the bad. Until the train shows her a slideshow of her decline. Then, she remembers. Every instance of the bad, in all its monstrousness. The bad men and the bad women who were her associates. The back-against-a-corner choices and the manipulation to undo them, only to make them again. If Lauren keeps going back, all the way back, she'll be back on a train that she came very close to never getting off of.

> *Perhaps a woman writhes in pain*
> *And listens—listens for the train!*
> *The train, that like an angel sings,*
> *The train, with healing on its wings.*

This stanza comes to Lauren from thin air, as if spoken over the train's loudspeaker. Lauren had believed she was healed, redeemed even, but here on this train, she feels like a ghost. Despite a front row seat to a silent movie of her past, she cannot reconcile the troubled girl from seven years ago with the woman she is today. That girl of skin and bones, who smelled always of sweat and chemicals, who wanted but one thing, is gone.

Where did my cell phone go? Lauren thinks. She doesn't see it, plunges her hand between the cushions again, and this time is rewarded. Her fingers clasp the cold plastic and she unearths the device. At first, Lauren thinks she's found someone else's phone, another traveler's lost-and-found. But then she recognizes it. This was her phone, seven years ago. It's an IPhone 3GS, the screen cracked from when she dropped it, drunk, outside the redbrick bar on the corner of Salem Street, the cobalt blue case scratched and scuffed. Lauren's fingers are so cold she fears they'll stick to the case like wet digits to an ice cube.

She types in her old passcode and the phone unlocks. Thumbing the contacts app open, she sees the last person she called, on August 5, 2009; the same as the last person she texted. The photos saved in the phone are snapshots from that humid summer morning in a city liquefying from the heat. Her hair is frizzy and her eyes are huge and glassy. In one sequence of photos, the strap of Lauren's tank top slips further and further down her shoulder in each shot. In another, Lauren has her arm around a man with haunted, disinterested eyes. Lauren throws the phone as if it's the bloodstained beak of a bird of prey, poised to peck her.

She hears a giggle and whips around. The woman and her daughter have returned. The little girl peeks out from behind her mother's skirts, feigning timidity. Over the woman's shoulder, Lauren sees a building that was demolished, more than five years ago, go whirring by, standing erect and reaching for the heavy clouds triumphantly.

"The engineer has rerouted us," the woman says.

"Who's the engineer?" Lauren asks. She tries not to let the fear creep into her voice but thinks maybe it does.

"The engineer steers the train," the woman says. She does not say anything else.

Lauren stands, wobbling on the wedged heels of her shoes after sitting for too long. She walks. Each car she passes through is dark and empty, but through the windows ahead, she sees a hazy, brassy light, as if they are coming up on an early morning horizon rather than driving straight into midnight. The empty cars wait to be filled, call out for passengers who are not there. Who will never be there.

Lauren crosses the threshold into the next car. The ceiling here feels too low and the ground is uneven. The walls of the train have been liberated from the laws of physics; they shiver and shake like trapped air beneath a downed parachute. Shadows darken the corners of Lauren's vision. Each time she turns her head to catch them, they move further away. Above these amorphous walls, the overhead racks are packed tight with luggage. Lauren reaches for the closest one and pulls. It clatters against an armrest before plummeting to the floor.

The sound of the zipper unzipping fills her with an obscure kind of dread. There are things in the suitcase, things she might have expected. Stolen things, from the past. Stolen things that have always been stolen. Money and razors, pistols and pocketknives, powders and pharmaceuticals, potions and poisons.

Lauren abandons the telltale suitcase. At the head of the car, someone has mounted the engineer's route on the wall. It's a huge map, the lines too big, the key too small. She follows the route with her finger, follows... follows... follows... The line glows menacingly, as if somewhere behind the map is a heat source of unpredictable power. As her finger traces the line to the end, the train lurches on its tracks. Lauren shudders and closes her eyes. Braces herself against the nebulous wall. Feels it shift beneath her hands. When she opens her eyes, she's standing in a steel room. Four walls, a ceiling, and floor of metal, gleaming like the end of a knife.

Lauren closes her eyes again and when she opens them, her steel prison is gone. She stands in a new car, one car back from where the engineer steers the train. Up ahead, she can see the silhouette of the engineer's hat bobbing to the motion of the train on its sparking tracks. A voice comes from behind her and Lauren lets out a cry.

The woman's daughter says, "My father drove our train into a cliff."

The flickering light casts shadows on her face so that Lauren can't quite tell what the girl is. Or isn't.

The woman says:

> *And smile, because she knows the train*
> *Has brought her children back again.*
> *We carry people home—and so*
> *God speeds us, wheresoe'er we go.*

Lauren watches shadows play across both of their faces now, turning them into animals or abstract paintings.

The little girl says, "My father was the engineer."

Lauren walks forward without consciously moving her feet.

The woman says, "*The End of the Line* is the last stop."

Lauren puts her hands over her ears. She does not want to go into the engineer's car, but when she concentrates all her efforts on stopping her feet from moving, the walls of the train move past her anyway. She is on a conveyor belt to Hell, but when Lauren arrives in the engineer's car, she finds there is no one there. The Devil is out to lunch.

A noise behind her.

"You're the engineer now," the woman shrieks and pushes Lauren onto the seat.

Lauren looks through a windshield marred by a thousand spider web cracks and sees the ruin. Sees the demolished wasteland. Sees the wreck of *The End of the Line*. She looks down for a key or a gearshift, but there's nothing. Only smooth, gleaming metal. When she looks up, the train is moving backwards, its wheels spinning at breakneck speeds.

"Where is this train going?" Lauren asks, her voice the quaking chirp of a sparrow, one that's flown headlong into latent glass. She trips on her long dress as she stands, rights herself, manages to take two tentative steps forward. "Why are we going backwards?"

"This train goes where I take it," the engineer says from Lauren's right. He sits in his engineer car at his engineer seat and tips her his engineer hat.

Lauren screams.

The train whistles.

Lauren begins to run.

The pattern of the carpet in the aisles shifts. It makes her dizzy. When she's lost count of the number of cars she's run through, Lauren slows. She looks up. The convex mirror, the other lidless eye of the monster who's been watching her travel through time, shows her who is sitting in the engineer's seat. It's her. Her emerald-amber eyes now the grey of twisted, smoking metal, and she's smiling a wicked smile at herself from under the brim of the engineer's hat.

Her hat.

When Lauren stops to think about it, she realizes that if she were to get off *The End of the Line*, it would somehow be seven years ago. She would either be getting off in the custody of police, doomed to repeat the familiar misery, a sentence as torturous as death itself. Or, she'd be getting off in a body bag. She hears the coroner zip the zipper. She feels the sensation of plastic against sweating skin, the sweat already beginning to cool.

"All passengers for Mysticism," the conductor calls from

somewhere unseen. "All for Mysticism!"

Lauren peers down the car to the exit. The woman steps into the aisle to block her view.

"You cannot get off," the woman says. "He needs you. He relies on you to navigate this train. We *all* need you now, to steer us along *The End of the Line*."

"To steer us along *The End of the Line!*" the little girl echoes. Her little girl lips are very red.

From somewhere on the train, someone laughs. Lauren thinks she sees the shadow of the engineer.

Lauren turns to the front of the train—or is it the back?

She begins to run.

THE ONE WHO ANSWERS THE DOOR

Harley reached for Zombie-Elsa's long blonde braid and tugged, her smile impish.

"Quit it." Zombie-Elsa adjusted her wig in the mirror. "You're on Mom's bad side for your slutty costume, so don't push your luck."

"It's not slutty," Harley Quinn said, surveying her appearance. "It's true to the comic. You're just jealous I picked it first."

The undead snow queen ignored this. "Hurry up. We're supposed to meet them in ten minutes. It'll take longer just to walk there."

Zombie-Elsa grabbed the icicle purse her sister had helped her splatter with fake blood the night before. They did not stop to say goodbye to their mother. Eleven and thirteen were too old to ask permission to go trick-or-treating.

They opened the door on the biting autumn air. The sun had succumbed to its washed-out cousin and the timing of its lunar phase meant a moon that hung low and large on the evening of All Hallows'.

The wind blew up tornadoes of leaves around their feet. Zombie-Elsa practiced her lumber, and giggled at her sister's attempts to execute a sexy slink. The sound was cut short by a scream.

A figure rushed Harley from the bushes. Harley gasped and jerked out of her attacker's reach, but the cape had already been lowered to reveal the grin beneath the eye mask.

"Gotcha!" Batgirl said. "You should have seen your face."

"There wasn't anything to see. You didn't scare me for shit," Harley countered.

"Just because you're wearing a disguise, doesn't mean you can swear." The voice was Zombie-Elsa's, but the words were their mother's.

"Hush up," Harley said. "Hey, where's—?"

"Carrie, the pyrotechnic prom queen?" came a voice from the shadows. A thin girl bathed in blood stepped out onto the road. "Right here."

"Cool costume," Zombie-Elsa said.

"Thanks," Carrie replied. She pinched a roll of nonexistent fat under her bloody prom dress. "I can't wait to eat oodles of candy. I've been dieting for weeks so I can cheat tonight. The houses in town better be ready to offer up the goods."

"We're skipping the houses in town tonight," Batgirl said.

"Why would we do that?" Harley asked.

"To trick-or-treat in Riverbend."

"What?" Zombie-Elsa squealed.

Harley held up her hand to silence her sister. She turned to Batgirl. "Why would we go to River's End?" she asked. Zombie-Elsa couldn't help but notice that she used the nickname the high school kids did when talking about the 'bend.

Batgirl shrugged. "The boys did it last year. They couldn't get Old Man Teasdale to open up his door to them. Bobby dared us to try this Halloween. We can't let those losers show us up. Although, I shouldn't call Bobby a loser since you totally have a crush on him. Unless..." Batgirl paused for emphasis. "You're too scared to go yourself."

"I'm not scared." Harley twirled a pigtail, defiance written between the white, blue, and pink lines of her carefully-applied makeup.

"Then what are we waiting for?" Batgirl asked, starting in the direction of Riverbend. Harley quickly followed, and Carrie fell in line without comment. Zombie-Elsa hurried to catch up with her sister, bombarding Harley with frantic questions.

"Shh," Harley hissed. "If you don't want to come, then go home."

Harley had also done a skillful job with Zombie-Elsa's

makeup, and beneath the white grease paint and black-red lipstick, Zombie-Elsa's frown was a grimace. She trotted behind her sister, wishing she'd worn sneakers under the long dress rather than the uncomfortable shoes that'd come with the costume.

A dense mist thickened the air, clinging to the foils and fabrics of the girls' costumes. By the time they'd walked beneath the archway marking the entrance to Riverbend, Zombie-Elsa's teeth were chattering. Her cape seemed little more than condensation-dampened saran wrap that would no longer stick. Batgirl led them deep into the 'bend. Zombie-Elsa saw Harley trying not to look at the residents' dwellings as they passed.

They walked without speaking. The only sound in the mist-muted night came from the leaves rustling in the trees. Batgirl stopped in front of a row of stone abodes and gestured at the first in the line. "This one. Miss Johnston's. Carrie, you knock first."

Carrie looked like someone had interrupted her prom queen acceptance speech with a cruel practical joke, but Batgirl's glare goaded her into action. She rapped three times, attempting to belie her apprehension with an indifferent smirk.

Seconds passed. A cloud smothered the moon.

"Looks like nobody's home," Batgirl chirped. Her eyes darted between slits of a mask that made her look more cunning raccoon than daring superhero. "Elsa, you're next. Susannah Pratchett's place."

"It's Zombie-Elsa. And no."

"No?"

"I don't want to."

"You have to," Batgirl said. "Otherwise, your sister has to knock on two."

Zombie-Elsa saw Harley's pale face grow paler. Perhaps thirteen wasn't so grownup after all.

"Fine," she said, approaching the intricately patterned door. She knocked a timid rat-a-tat-tat.

When no one answered, she breathed out a sigh she hadn't realized she'd been holding prisoner. *I wonder if these edifices hold other things prisoner.* She shook the thought from her head and gave Batgirl a triumphant look.

"My turn," Batgirl said, unimpressed. She strode up to the fortress at the top of a steep stone staircase and banged on the door loud enough to wake the dead.

They waited.

For one dread-filled moment, Zombie-Elsa thought she heard the grating sound of scraping stone. She tensed, fearing the worst.

The door remained closed.

Batgirl tried to hide her relief, but the fingers that clutched the straps of her bag were white-knuckled, and shook ever-so-slightly.

Batgirl turned on Harley, hands on hips, regaining her earlier arrogance. "Last one," she said, moving down the dirt path. She pointed to the largest structure and grinned, a wide-mouthed, Jack-o-lantern grin. "There. Old Man Teasdale."

Everyone knew the story of how Old Man Teasdale had come by such a foreboding residence. According to the legend, the farmer had grown tired of providing for his family and banished them from his property at the start of a bitter, snowy winter. Only one of the relatives survived, Teasdale's daughter, and when the day finally came on which she could exact her revenge, she had her father removed from the farm and exiled to the stone house in Riverbend.

The dwelling was designed to keep in what shouldn't be allowed out. Granite vines crawled up the walls, and weatherworn pillars encircled the property like road signs for a neighborhood in the land of the dead. Fiendish angels held vigil at either side of the ivy-choked doorway and granite vases of desiccated flowers bookended the leaf-littered stoop.

Zombie-Elsa watched as Harley pursed her lips and stepped forward. She wanted to stop her, wanted to take her sister's hand and run all the way home, locking the door behind them. There would be other dares, she wanted to tell her. Other boys to impress. But Zombie-Elsa could tell that Bobby was the furthest thing from Harley's mind as she approached that terrible, waiting door. It stretched up, yawning before her. Zombie-Elsa imagined vampiric teeth springing from its hinges to bite her sister's fingers.

Harley Quinn reached a trembling hand toward the door. She knocked once, twice, three times, on the stone panel. The echoes continued on, like the beating of the Tell-Tale Heart.

The crypt door swung open.

FLOWERS FROM AMARYLLIS

You step onto the ward with your densely-bandaged wrists and your hollow, haunted gaze and you don't look into a single friendly face upon being introduced. Your hair was once the color of wheat beneath a noon-day sun, but has faded to a brown the shade of timid rabbits in a shadowed thicket. As soon as you're able, you retreat into the room you've been assigned, and don't come out for the rest of that night, the next day, or the following evening. At almost midnight on what will be your third day on the ward, you pitter-pat out in your hospital garb and tangled hair, and you shake and sob and tell the nightshift nurse that there's someone in your room.

"Of course there's someone in your room. Two someones to be exact," the nurse says. "Your roommates, Olive and Lauren."

You are inconsolable, and the nurse softens, offers you something to help you sleep. You place your Elavil and your substantial dose of Valium upon your tongue, and on the way back in to make bargains with the Sandman, you mutter something that sounds like, *please let it be gone.*

On your fifth day on the ward, your former foster parents try to visit, but you deny them entry (*why won't they cut you off, the way Imogene has?*), and the staff has no choice but to obey your wishes. Outside the locked doors, in the cramped anteroom where an ancient elevator chimes regardless of whether or not the call button has been pressed, the woman who did all she could to mother you after your parents were killed stands, crying and pleading to be able to see you.

The mental health clinician, Lisa, a patient woman who elicits understanding from even the most distressed of visitors, convinces Sheila Gonzalez that you are being well-taken care of, and that if there's anything she'd like to leave for you—clothes or candy, books or playing cards—she can do so, and you'll have access to it as soon as it undergoes the requisite contraband check. Sheila visibly brightens, turns to Ray Gonzalez, slight and silent at the corner of the anteroom, and gestures for him to give her what he holds between his hands.

It's a decorative fabric box, the kind for storing photos in, and Lisa takes it, tells Sheila and Ray that they should call tomorrow, that perhaps you will be ready to speak to them then.

"Before we go, can you tell me, has our daughter's wife, Imogene, been to see her yet?"

Lisa tells Sheila that by some strange stroke of misfortune, each instance of Imogene's arrival has seen you off the ward for one medical test or another.

"Make sure Willow knows," Sheila implores. "She's convinced her struggles will lead those who love her to abandon her, but Imogene's not going anywhere, and neither are we."

The visiting hour is hectic and the box of photographs is forgotten until the following morning, when your doctor arrives for the day's appointments. You are third on his list, which means you are pulled from a group on relaxation and deep breathing exercises, though neither tactic has had any effect on your state of mind. You trudge into the office with the enthusiasm of a cat before a bath and sit on the edge of the chair, your body language a testament to your distrust and exhaustion.

After questions about your meds (you feel lethargic), how you're eating (you're not), and how you're sleeping (in fits and starts, for fifteen minutes or so each hour), the doctor asks if you would like to go through the photographs that your once-foster parents delivered.

You bristle, but Dr. Mendelevitch explains that the duration of your stay depends on the effort put into your treatment, and so with pursed lips and a shrug, you agree and brace for this Rorschach test of images rather than cnidarian blobs of ink.

The doctor lifts the stack of photographs from the box

and unties the salmon, satin ribbon keeping them in place. On the desk, he fans them out like he's reviewing paint samples, plucks up a single photograph, studies it, then turns it so it's facing you. A long-taloned hand reaches up from the depths of your empty stomach to grab you by the throat. In the photo, you are fifteen...

—

You are fifteen, and it is the evening of your sophomore homecoming dance. Neither your mother nor your father has a sharp word or worried glance at the news that you are going with Imogene Rogers.

"I love you no matter what," your father says, and you warm with the knowledge that all is, and will continue to be, right with the world.

When Imogene arrives, your mother stitches a tear in the girl's hem, while you make last minute adjustments to your cat-eye liner and Heidi-braid. Your father takes rapid-fire shots of you and Imogene until you smile shyly, kiss Imogene on the cheek, and ask your date if she'll take a picture of you and your parents. Imogene counts to three, you squeeze your parents' hands with each of your own, and your smile is like a spray of tulips at the start of April, blooming toward the flash of light.

No one snaps a picture of you at your parents' funeral the following week. If they had, any beholder would think your lips incapable of flowering smiles or kisses.

—

When Dr. Mendelevitch lowers the photo, you are looking out the room's one barred window. Your hands are shaking, and you struggle to clasp them in your lap around the bulky bandages encircling your wrists.

The doctor squints at the computer screen. "I see you've been treated for an irregular heartbeat and electrolyte imbalances in the past. During these prior hospitalizations, you were identified as a suicide risk due to the nature of your self-inflicted wounds. Did these behaviors begin immediately after the death of your parents?"

Your eyes do not stray from the window. A seagull soars past the glass, and you visualize the sandy beach to which it is traveling, the algae-slick rocks above the crashing surf on which it will perch.

"Willow?"

You drag your gaze away from the outside world and back to the doctor as if you've lived out five hundred lives on the ward since Friday, as if the first of the photographs has had a vampiric effect on your vitality.

"Maybe we should move on to the next photo," Dr. Mendelevitch says.

You nod, emit a small exhalation of relief.

"What can you tell me about this one?"

The memory associated with the photo leeches what little color was left in your face. You remember that day, the storm, your vision swimming along a horizon that surged like a gale-ravaged sea. You remember the seismic wave of nausea; you remember stopping to lift the tangle of hair from your neck, and strain to hear past the ringing in your ears. The thunder is closer now, a hornets' nest knocked from the eaves and rolling, helter-skelter, down the sidewalk. You are nineteen...

—

You are nineteen, and days pass with all the detail of half-finished pencil sketches, grey and smudged and evanescent. You have been living from acquaintances' couches to shelters and back again for three years now, unwilling to burden Sheila, Ray, and Imogene with your defectiveness any longer. It is easier this way, easier to subject your body to the repertoire of tortures it requires. Food is scarce and instruments of pain abound in the absence of everything else.

On the day you are caught in the storm, you have not eaten in over a week. Though indiscriminate shapes bob at your periphery, the shadow wolf is unmistakable. It's been stalking you since the night of the accident, the night a young man's negligence cost your parents everything. Nineteen of Keith Coates' driving citations had been covered up by his father, a local senator. The twentieth was a head-on collision with your parents' Prius.

You will never put the ones who love you in the position of wishing they hadn't given you a second chance. Maybe the shadow wolf is real, and maybe it's a manifestation of your fractured mind; either way, you will not string your family along while you do what needs to be done to escape it.

The rain increases from a drizzle to a deluge, and, unexpectedly, the front bedroom of the Gonzalez's warm, inviting home flashes across your mind's eye with a corresponding zigzag of lightening. You shake the image of this place you have abandoned from your head, and turn to put some distance between you and the shadow wolf.

You stop at the sound of a whimper on the wind.

You can make little sense of a tiny foxhound puppy

beneath the verdant stalks of a plot of amaryllises, but a flourishing garden in this neighborhood of debris-strewn lawns and boarded-up windows is equally perplexing. You bring the puppy to your chest, and its quivering body is like fur-covered twigs tossed together by the storm. You set your jaw and focus your gaze, preparing to outrun the shadow wolf.

When you look over your shoulder to gauge the distance between you, its sinister presence is gone.

It is only later, of course, that the picture is taken. Euphoric at your return, frantic to feed both the foster daughter who left and the malnourished puppy she has returned with, Sheila Gonzalez sets you up at the kitchen table with a massive plate of food and snaps a photo on her old Minolta camera without warning.

The black and white film cannot soften the angles of your cheeks, or the depressions beneath your eyes, but it does capture something else. The tilt of your jaw is like a daylily in fall, set against the wind, confirmation that the shadow wolf did not destroy you, that deliverance is at hand.

You name the puppy Amaryllis, after the flowers under which you found her. Perhaps it is only a coincidence that they were your mother's favorites.

—

A knock comes at the door, and the nurse who opens it doesn't bother to hide her annoyance at Dr. Mendelevitch and his lack of progress on the day's appointments. The doctor shoos her away with an impatient gesture. His movements cause the satin ribbon to cascade over the side of his desk like molten lava over a volcano summit. The doctor nabs the end of the ribbon right before it is lost, and you ask if you can hold it. Dr. Mendelevitch wavers.

"Just while I'm in your office," you say. "I know we can't have anything resembling rope on the ward."

He smiles at your insight, passes over the ribbon. You run it through your fingers, tie it in a bow around the arm of the chair, the way you used to around Amaryllis' neck. The dog would prance as if the Gonzalez's living room was the Westminster Kennel Club arena, velvet ears falling back from her delicately-boned face, tail drumming a beat against the side of Ray's leather armchair.

"Your last hospitalization..." Dr. Mendelevitch pauses to calculate forward from the date scrawled on the back of the photo he still held, "was a little over a year after this was taken."

You think, *the duration of your stay depends on the effort put into your treatment*, and therefore say, "The shadow wolf stopped chasing me when I found Amaryllis. It took a little while for my body to acknowledge this."

"The... shadow wolf? Can you tell me more about that?"

The shadow of another bird passes the glass and you fight the urge to surrender to the pull of the world outside the window. "I... it's hard to explain. I saw it for the first time the night my parents died. The last time was the day of the thunderstorm. The day I found Amaryllis. Now that she's... it's come back. It's always been hard to see head-on. Mostly it stays at one corner of my vision. But it is always there.

"Imogene doesn't understand. She thinks if I surround myself with people who support me, or go into treatment, I'll get better. It's when I..." you pause, swallow, "don't eat, or when I cut myself, that it stays away. That's why I was admitted. I wasn't trying to kill myself, I just... I was trying to make the darkness go away."

You weave the ribbon between your fingers, then stop and gesture rather wildly toward the desk. "Which photo's next, Doctor? The one of Sheila jumping for joy when I got my GED? How about Imogene in her florist apron, the day I ran into her at the local nursery and we started spending time together again? I took a lot of those photographs myself, you know. I even worked as a photographer for the local paper. Imogene convinced me to get into it."

Dr. Mendelevitch holds up another photo. "Is this Imogene?" he asks.

You wilt like wisteria in winter at the image before you, at how blindingly white your wedding dresses were in the camera's flash. You can make out the amaryllises along the dance floor in one corner of the shot, and you run your tongue over your lips in hopes of tasting the ghost of the decadent frosting that topped your raspberry crème cake.

"We have each other now," Imogene had said, as she'd looked into your eyes and gripped you tight. "And we will always have each other, for I will never leave you, Willow..."

But she had left, hadn't she?

"Yes. That's her." You are suddenly tired enough that departing this office and journeying back to your bed seems like an endeavor requiring far more stamina than you possess.

Dr. Mendelevitch straightens the photos and returns them to the box. "Have you talked to Imogene since you were admitted?"

"Imogene will not be coming to see me."

The doctor looks back at his computer screen, confused. "It says here that your wife has been to the ward several times. Once you were having your wrists rebandaged, another instance you were on the Cardiology floor having an EKG, and the third time she visited, you were with the chaplain."

"The nurses and counselors are telling me that to keep my spirits up. I know they're lying." You hold out the ribbon with a look that says the ribbon is the only other thing the doctor will be getting from you, and think, whether they keep you here longer or not, that enough effort has been put into your treatment for one day. "Are we done?"

Dr. Mendelevitch sighs. "We certainly don't have time for me to challenge these iterations of delusional thinking, Ms. Keret, so I suppose we're through. I would like to try you on a new medication, however. Something for hallucinations. Let's see if we can't get this shadow creature to go up in smoke, shall we?"

You make a gesture somewhere between acquiescence and apathy, and the placid look on the doctor's face as he enters the pharmacy order tells you that despite your swift consent, you have not aroused his suspicion.

—

You wait until two-fifteen AM, when the last three instances of checks have produced neither sigh nor stirring on the part of your roommates'. You extricate yourself from the web of tangled sheets and open the nightstand drawer, pausing when it creaks. Olive and Lauren stay asleep. You retrieve the small bouquet of origami roses—the sweet schizophrenic who'd lived in Japan for several years made them for you when you mentioned you loved flowers in an arts and crafts group—and shake the bouquet upside down over your lap.

Ten Elavil and ten Valium tablets, two each for each of the days you've been on the ward, two per paper rose, rain down like sweets from a candy-store dispenser, amassed the way a child would sneak candy from a discerning parent, held beneath the tongue until around the corner and out of sight. You hold the twenty pills in your palm, and you think of what you have lost, of how you have come to the end of your ability to cope with the unfairness, and with pain.

You lift your hand to your lips, drop the pills into your mouth like seeds, and wait for them to take root.

—

Following irrevocability such as this, you assumed that the shadow wolf would dissipate like fog off the sea, but it looms from the corner, gnashing its teeth as your breathing slows, striking forward while your pillow loses solidity. You can feel it, its waves and billows replete with cloying substance that leaves condensation on your greying skin. You smell it, the dank, heavy scent of impending death. You hear... clicking.

Clicking like the sound of toenails on linoleum. With a burst of strength—your last—you turn your head, and are overwrought by what you see. Amaryllis, halfway across the room, the fur on her back raised in warning. She stalks toward the shadow wolf, and you blink; your vision recalibrates like the autofocus on a camera, and you determine that it is not Amaryllis. It couldn't be. This dog is smaller, speckled.

The therapy dog, then. Poppy, or Posey... something like that.
A beagle, not a foxhound. Although...

The dog bears down upon the shadow wolf, and though your perception flickers, you are able to focus a final, fleeting moment. You descry the dog's eyes. Amaryllis' eyes, deep brown with flecks of amber. The eyes you looked into every day for fifteen years, and that mirrored your flowering and your fortitude back to you.

You struggle for enough breath to say her name. It dies in your throat like a poison-doused perennial.

—

It does not surprise you that whatever afterlife you assume you've entered into is rife with the smell of amaryllises; like your mother, they have always been your favorite. You are bewildered, however, by the persistence of pain. You strain to swallow around the tube in your throat, open your eyes, and see the hospital room around you.

It is different from the room to which you were assigned on the ward. The sunlight offered up by a window the width of the space sets the glass-vased amaryllises on fire. You attempt to sit up, are stopped by the innumerable wires twining your body like ivy. Before you can panic, a nurse appears at your elbow, and places a hand on your still-bandaged wrist.

"Relax, honey, you're in the ICU. You're going to be okay."

She replaces one IV bag with another, and you feel a narcotic soothing of your anxiety.

"You are lucky," she says, "though they still can't figure out what happened. Nurses on the ward heard barking coming from your room. When they got there, they found you blue, not breathing. It was only later, when they'd gotten you to the ER, that they realized they never saw a dog."

Twice now, that Amaryllis has thought you worth saving. Or, perhaps, it has been countless times, one for each of the days she was with you, making you whole, making you better.

Perhaps you can be made better once again.

The nurse studies you, finds your dropping blood pressure and stabilized breathing satisfying enough to make her way toward the door.

When you wake again, the light is softer, more diffuse, like yellow begonias at dusk. The pinch at the back of your throat is gone and you can turn your head, now that you have been freed from some of the creeping tubes and climbing wires.

Imogene sits in a sage-green chair, her black hair cut shorter than you can ever remember seeing it. At first, you think she's sleeping, but she shifts, and you realize it was a trick of the fading sunlight, casting shadows where none should be.

The amaryllises she holds are a deeper red than any of the other bouquets. Her wedding ring shimmers, diamond-white and sapphire in the light. You hold each other's gaze.

Imogene is here. She has not left. Like Amaryllis, she continues to think you worth saving.

The sun dips below the horizon. Shadows emerge from corners and spread throughout the room, but they are none of them wolf-like, none of them more sinister than any other image cast upon the ground, intercepting light.

Imogene's lips part in a smile, chrysanthemums

embracing the sweetness of the changing season.

Your mouth responds in turn.

You smile at one another. Your smiles are two gardens, and the moss-covered walls around them have begun to crumble.

REFERENCES

Kilmer, Joyce. "The Twelve Forty-Five." *The Complete Poems of Joyce Kilmer*. Kindle Edition, JR Publishing [Public Domain], April 20, 2012, pp. 6-8.

ACKNOWLEDGEMENTS

Something Borrowed, Something Blood-Soaked represents both my life and my writing post-recovery from addiction, so in many instances, the people I'm thanking for their assistance in crafting my fiction are also the ones who've had a hand in helping me maintain my sobriety (whether they know it or not). Subsequently, my gratitude for these individuals is boundless and profound.

To my mother and father, Jeanne and Rick, thank you for being the most loving, supportive, and encouraging parents a girl could ask for. Everything I've ever been able to accomplish has been because of your belief in me. To my sister, Lauren, who displays my horror anthologies on the desk at her prestigious Miami law firm, no matter how gory or gruesome the cover... I love you, Shashu Ba-bay!

To my wonderful husband, John, who begins most evenings by asking me, "Do you still have writing to do?" and is patient, supportive, and understanding, regardless of what the answer is (it's usually, 'yes'). A line from "The Girl Who Loved Bruce Campbell" seems fitting here: "You're cute, babe. I love that you love blood and guts as much as I do."

To *Unnerving* editor/publisher, Eddie Generous, thank you first for publishing "Red Room" in *Unnerving Magazine* Issue #5, and second, for being such a beast of an avid reader—consuming mainstream and indie horror fiction with inhuman consistency—and listening to the *Tales to Terrify* podcast episode that featured the short story version of the "Liquid Handcuffs" novella in this collection. That this helped convince you to publish *Something Borrowed...* tickles me pink as the pig on the haunting, hypnotizing cover you designed. Your work ethic is contagious, and it's an honor to be among your 2018 catalogue of authors.

Thank you to Stephanie M. Wytovich, Ben Eads, and Joe Mynhardt of Crystal Lake Publishing. The insight with which you provided me over the course of my mentorship was invaluable, and I will carry your professionalism, enthusiasm, and expertise with me wherever I go in my career.

Thank you to Jessica Wick for convening each week for Writing Day, and for your help with a great many of these stories, from listening to "Thirsty Creatures" at Open Mic Night to beta reading "Red Room" and providing last-minute edits on "Flowers from Amaryllis."

Julia Rios, thank for driving all the way to Westerly for Writing Day! Thank you for your keen eye for detail, for your assumption that I'd have some Halloween-inspired flash fiction lying around, and for publishing the eponymous story of this collection in *Fireside Fiction*. Not only does my work always get stronger after we've toiled through something together, but we have a grand old time in the process... amirite, bears?

I think the Savoy Bookshop and Café had been open for all of five minutes when I materialized before Event Coordinator Elissa Englund-Sweet, introduced myself as a local 'writer,' despite having but a handful of publishing credits to my name, and started chatting about upcoming events and local authors. Thank you for seeing my mildly manic enthusiasm for what it was: unadulterated excitement at having a bookstore—and book-minded people—in a town that can sometimes feel light-years away from the bibliophilic culture of a bigger city. Your friendship and the introductions you facilitated to other writers in the community have been my saving grace since returning to Westerly.

Thank you to Claire Cooney, the first writer Elissa put me in touch with, and a gracious, graceful, and inspirational human being. Thank you for your advice, your time, your passion, and most of all, thank you for being an enchanted beacon of light and creativity.

I was struck with a lethal bout of imposter syndrome upon having this collection accepted for publication. Soon after, Carlos Hernandez provided me with a letter of recommendation for several MFA programs I was applying to. Your generous praise of my work, and acknowledgment of my ambition, helped me overcome that self-doubt, and your ongoing support is unparalleled.

Thank you to my original 'editor,' Lazaryn McLaughlin, i.e., the first person besides my immediate family members who showed any interest in my stories, even the early, less-than-stellar ones.

Thank you to Sarah Itteilag for never batting an eye at the text messages I've sent, texts that, in requesting her nursing expertise, must seem like I'm either planning a murder, or have just committed one.

Thank you to the astoundingly talented, remarkable women who blurbed this collection: Gwendolyn Kiste, Stephanie M. Wytovich, Christina Sng, and Jessica McHugh. I am in awe of your collective body of work, and am inspired daily by your commitment to your craft.

Hearty thank-yous to Juliana Rew, George Somers, Randy Chandler & Cheryl Mullenax of Comet Press, E.J. Wentstrom, Anna Reith, Shane Staley, Scott Silk, Weasel "The Dude," of Weasel Press, Brett Pribble, D Chang of Space Squid, for first publishing ten of these thirteen stories.

Thank you to Sarah Cleto and Brittany Warmen for the feedback on "Wolves at the Door..." at the culmination of a magical Carterhaugh School of Folklore and the Fantastic Legends course, and to my fellow students in the Harvard Extension School's Creative Writing and Literature Master's Program for critiquing additional drafts of that same story.

Lastly, and perhaps needlessly, for she has no reason to pick up this book, having lived the inspiration for each of these stories with me (and, well, the whole no opposable thumbs thing), a thank you to my Maya Bear for remaining faithfully by my side, ever patient while I click away at my keyboard or stare off into space, letting me know when it's time to take a break for dinner or a walk outside. She is my Amaryllis, my expanse of flowers after the rain, the light that chases the shadow wolf away.

And the shadows do come, no matter the pains we take

to keep them at bay. A final thank-you to the reader who picks up this book, and finds something within its pages to shed light on their own shadow wolf. Those things have teeth, but they back down quickly when you show a little mettle.

Christa Carmen,
May 1, 2018